Making Mischief with Jeremy James

David Henry Wilson was born in London in 1937 and educated at Dulwich College and Pembroke College, Cambridge. Before retirement, he lectured at the universities of Bristol and Konstanz, Germany, where he founded the student theatre. His plays have been widely performed in England, America, Germany and Scandinavia, and his children's books – especially the Jeremy James series – have been translated into several languages. His novel *The Coachman Rat* has been acclaimed in England, America and Germany. He is married with three grown-up children and lives in Taunton, Somerset.

Making Mischief with Jeremy James

with

David Henry Wilson

Illustrated by Axel Scheffler

MACMILLAN CHILDREN'S BOOKS

Do Gerbils Go to Heaven? first published 1996 by Macmillan Children's Books
Never Steal Wheels from a Dog first published 2001 by Macmillan Children's Books

This edition published 2008 by Macmillan Children's Books
a division of Macmillan Publishers Limited
20 New Wharf Road, London N1 9RR
Basingstoke and Oxford
Associated companies throughout the world
www.panmacmillan.com

ISBN 978-0-330-45277-9

1 3 5 7 9 8 6 4 2

A CIP catalogue record for this book is available from
the British Library.

Typeset by Intype Libra Limited
Printed and bound in the UK by CPI Mackays, Chatham ME5 8TD

Do Gerbils Go to Heaven?

In memory of Herta Ryder,
who was special

Contents

CHAPTER ONE

Hospital Fish

The entrance to the hospital was a big glass door, which suddenly split into two. Through the middle came Mummy, wheeling Christopher and Jennifer in their pushchair, and Jeremy James, who was holding his left wrist in his right hand. They all went across a large room to a sort of counter where a grey-haired lady sat writing in a book.

"Hello," said the grey-haired lady, looking up.

"Hello," said Mummy, looking down.

"What lovely children!" said the grey-haired lady.

Jeremy James wasn't feeling lovely. He was feeling painful – or to be more precise, his left wrist was feeling painful. He'd fallen off his tricycle and, as Daddy was away trying to find London, Mummy had brought him to the Accident Centre.

"This is the patient," said Mummy, and the lady looked down at Jeremy James.

"Oh dear," she said. "And what have you done, young man?"

The young man told her what he'd done, so she

took down the details and asked Mummy to wait while she told the doctor.

Mummy, Jeremy James and the twins sat down near an elderly man with bristles and an elderly woman with a stick.

"Injured yerself, 'ave yer?" asked the man.

"Yes," said Jeremy James. "I've hurt my wrist. I fell off my tricycle."

The man said that his wife had hurt her ankle.

"Did she fall off her tricycle as well?" asked Jeremy James.

"No, she ain't learned ter drive," said the man. "She caught 'er foot in the carpet."

Jeremy James said he'd caught fish in the river and flu from liquorice allsorts, but he'd never caught a foot in a carpet.

"What did she catch it with?" he asked.

" 'er leg," said the man.

Just then a young, rosy-cheeked lady in a blue uniform came across, and Jeremy James had to go with her to see the doctor.

The doctor had a white coat, thinning red hair, twinkling blue eyes, and a painful way of waggling Jeremy James's left wrist.

"Does that hurt?" he asked.

"Owowow!" said Jeremy James.

"That sounds like yes," said the doctor. "Let's get it X-rayed, shall we?"

"What's an eggs-ray?" asked Jeremy James.

The doctor explained that it was a picture which

2

3

showed if your bone was broken. Now Jeremy James had seen broken toys and broken vases and all the things Daddy broke when he was doing repairs, and so he told the doctor that his wrist wasn't broken. The doctor was a little surprised.

"How do you know?" he asked.

"Because if it was," said Jeremy James, "my hand would have fallen off."

Nevertheless, the rosy nurse took Jeremy James along a corridor, round a bend, along another corridor, through some glass doors, and down a passage. He saw lots of doors and windows, a wheelchair here, a trolley there, a man on crutches, a woman in a dressing-gown, a man in a white coat, and a very interesting fish-tank with fish and bubbles and bits of green. He would have liked to have a closer look at the fish-tank, but the nurse was hurrying along, and so he hurried along with her.

When they came to the X-ray department, the nurse handed him over to another young lady with glasses and a tightly tied pigtail.

"Yes, I'll look after him," said the pigtailed lady. "Just wait here, Jeremy James, and I'll come for you as soon as I'm ready."

She disappeared into a dark room, and closed the door. Jeremy James sat on a red chair, and looked around. There were three other chairs, all empty, a little table with some old magazines, and nothing and nobody else.

Jeremy James's thoughts turned to the fish-tank.

Now *that* would be interesting. He wouldn't mind waiting for the pigtailed lady at the fish-tank, because then he'd have something to look at. Fish, for instance. And after all, the pigtailed lady had said she'd come for him when she was ready, and it wouldn't make any difference to her if he was sitting in a red chair or standing beside a fish-tank.

Jeremy James gently slid off the chair, taking care not to bump his damaged wrist, and set off up the passage towards the glass doors. On the other side of these were several corridors that went in different directions, but he was pretty sure that the fish-tank was along *that* corridor, and so *that* was the corridor he took.

The fish-tank wasn't along *that* corridor. There were doors, windows, a long-haired young man who said hello, a bald-headed man who didn't say hello, and a fat lady with a thin broom.

Maybe the fish-tank was along *this* corridor . . . No, there didn't seem to be anything at all along *this* corridor . . . In fact *this* corridor just led to another corridor, but at least there was someone in the other corridor – a lady pushing a trolly of tea and sand-wiches.

"Excuse me," said Jeremy James.

"Hello, dear," said the lady.

"Can you tell me the way to the fish-tank?"

"Fish-tank?" exclaimed the lady. "You won't find no fish-tank here, dear, this is a hospital."

"There *is* a fish-tank, because I've seen it!" said Jeremy James.

"Then it must be in the kitchen," said the lady. "Just go down the corridor, and turn to the right. That way . . ."

She pointed.

"Thank you!" said Jeremy James.

"Here," she said. "Have a piece o' fruit cake."

Jeremy James thanked her even more, and with fruit cake in hand and mouth set off down the corridor. The lady watched him go, shook her head, and pushed her trolley through a swing door, muttering, "Fish-tank. I never seen no fish-tank. I thought they got their fish from the fishmonger."

The kitchen was full of pots and pans and big ovens and steam and people in white coats and hats.

"Hullo, there!" said a red-faced, black-moustached, bushy-browed man. "Enjoying our fruit cake?"

"Yes, thank you," said Jeremy James.

"Then have another piece."

Jeremy James didn't say no.

"Visiting somebody, are you?"

"No," said Jeremy James. "I've hurt my wrist."

"Didn't think our fruit cake was that heavy," said the man. "Where's your mother, sonny?"

"She's over there," said Jeremy James, vaguely waving his fruit-cake-holding hand. "With Christopher and Jennifer."

"Ah," said the man.

6

"Can you tell me where the fish-tank is?" asked Jeremy James.

"What fish-tank?" asked the man.

"The one with fish in it," said Jeremy James.

"Anybody seen a fish-tank?" the man called out.

"Try the fishiotherapy department," said a white-hatted man.

Meanwhile, the young lady with glasses and the tight pigtail had said goodbye to a fair-haired man with an ear-ring and a limp, and was gazing at the empty red chair on which Jeremy James had been but was no longer sitting.

"Oh!" she said.

She looked up the corridor, looked down the corridor, looked right, looked left, said "Oh!" again, called out "Jeremy James!" a few times, and then stood still and thought. Perhaps the boy had gone back to his mother in the waiting-room.

She hurried to the waiting-room, but there was no sign of Jeremy James. A lady was sitting there with two toddlers, and the grey-haired receptionist confirmed that that was Jeremy James's mother.

The receptionist and the pigtailed lady whispered to each other:

"Should I tell her?"

"Well, I don't know. Don't want to worry her."

"Supposing we can't find him?"

"He must be somewhere."

"Supposing he's been kidnapped?"

In the end they decided that the pigtailed lady

should organize a search, and the receptionist should tell Jeremy James's mother.

Before long, there were nurses, porters, and even patients going round asking if anyone had seen a little boy wearing a smart red pullover and holding his left wrist in his right hand. Quite a lot of people had seen him: a young man with long hair remembered saying hello to him, a lady with a trolley had given him some fruit cake, the cooks in the kitchen had given him more fruit cake, and a doctor and two nurses and three visitors and four patients had all seen him at different times and in different places. But where was he now? Nobody knew. The only clue was that he'd been asking for the fish-tank.

The pigtailed lady knew all about the fish-tank, and her hopes leapt like a salmon, but when she got there, her hopes sank like a brick. The fish were there, but Jeremy James wasn't.

Then an old lady said she'd seen a little boy walking hand in hand with a man in overalls, and they'd left the hospital. She couldn't remember what the little boy was wearing, but it *might* have been a red pullover.

At this news the pigtailed lady burst into tears, and a doctor said it was time to send for the police, and the grey-haired receptionist told Mummy not to worry, and messages were sent to every ward and every department, and several porters went out to search the car-parks and the gardens.

Meanwhile, Jeremy James had wandered through

an open double-door and found himself in a large, bright room. There were colourful pictures on the walls, two tables with toy telephones, a rocking-horse with a little girl on it, a tank with a little boy in it, a doll's house, a slide, and more toys and more children.

"Hello," said a boy the same age and size as Jeremy James.

"Hello," said Jeremy James.

"Would you like to play telephones with me?"

"Yes, please," said Jeremy James. "Only I've got to have an egg-ray when the pigtailed lady comes."

The other boy, whose name was Simon, said he'd just had a sandwich and some fruit cake, and he didn't think he could eat an egg-ray on top of all that.

9

With all the wandering and fish-hunting and fruit cake-eating, Jeremy James was beginning to feel quite warm, and so very carefully, so as not to hurt his wrist, he took off his red pullover, and put it on the floor under a chair. Then he and Simon sat at the tables with the toy telephones.

At that moment a round-faced smiley nurse poked her head round a door and called out: "Everybody all right?"

A chorus of voices cried: "Yes, thank you, Nurse Baker!"

"Good!" said Nurse Baker, and went back into the ward just as one of the porters entered.

"You 'aven't seen a little boy wearin' a red pullover, 'ave yer?" he asked.

"No," said Nurse Baker.

"I s'pose 'e might be in the playroom," said the porter.

"I've just been in there," said Nurse Baker, "and there's certainly no one in a red pullover."

"Ah well, 'e must be somewhere else," said the porter.

By now the the police had arrived, and while Jeremy James was dialling 999 to talk to Simon, Mummy was giving a policeman a detailed description of Jeremy James. Another policeman was talking to the old lady who'd seen the boy with the man in the overalls. Someone else had also seen them, and the boy had been wearing a brown jacket, had swung his left arm, and had called the man Daddy.

10

"Then maybe he was a different boy," said the old lady.

Jeremy James might well have stayed in the play-room for the rest of the day, and maybe even the night as well, if at that moment Simon's mummy and daddy hadn't happened to come in to see their son. First they said hello to Simon, and then they said hello to his new friend, and when they asked the new friend what his name was, Simon's mummy said:

"Isn't that the little boy they're all looking for?"

"Can't be," said Simon's daddy. "He's supposed to be wearing a red pullover."

"*I've* got a red pullover," said Jeremy James, and pulled it out from under the chair to show them.

"Then you're the one they're looking for," said Simon's daddy.

There was quite a lot of fuss when Jeremy James was finally taken back to see Mummy and the twins. The rosy-cheeked nurse and the pigtailed lady were in tears, the grey-haired receptionist was smiling, two doctors and two policemen were frowning, Jennifer was laughing, Christopher was crying, and Mummy had a sort of pleased-to-see-you-but-where-have-you-been look on her face.

Jeremy James found it all rather puzzling, and told Mummy about the fish-tank and the fruit cake and the toy telephones.

One of the policemen took notes, and murmured

as he wrote: "Fish-tank ... fruit cake ... toy telephones ... Crime o' the century."

Eventually, the policemen said goodbye, the doctors and nurses went back to work, and Jeremy James walked with his right hand in the hand of the pigtailed lady all the way to the X-Ray room. And when she'd finished taking the X-Ray, she held his hand all the way back to the waiting-room.

It turned out that Jeremy James had been right. His wrist wasn't broken. The doctor with the thinning red hair and the now-not-quite-so-twinkling blue eyes said it was just a sprain, and the now-extremely-rosy-cheeked nurse put a bandage on it.

There were more goodbyes, and at last Mummy, Jeremy James and the twins slowly made their way towards the big glass doors that self-opened and self-closed. But before they got there, Jeremy James stopped and looked up at Mummy.

"Mummy," he said.

"What is it, Jeremy James?" asked Mummy.

"Before we leave, please can we see the fish-tank?"

"No!" said Mummy.

Jeremy James couldn't understand why Mummy said it so sharply.

CHAPTER TWO

The Greatest Game

"I've been to lots of hospitals," said Timothy. "I've been to lots more hospitals than you'll ever go to."

"Well I've only ever been to one," said Jeremy James.

"And I've been to lots," said Timothy.

Timothy was the red-haired, freckle-faced boy from the big house next door, and he had not only been everywhere, but he had also done everything and knew everyone.

"What's the matter with you, then?" asked Jeremy James.

"Nothing's the matter with me," said Timothy. "I'm perfect."

"But people only go to hospital if they're ill," said Jeremy James. "Like me, with my pained wrist."

"I've had lots of pained wrists," said Timothy.

"You can't have lots," said Jeremy James, "because you've only got two wrists."

"I've had lots," said Timothy. "And I've had bigger bandages than that. I've had bandages all over my hand *and* my arm."

They were sitting on the lawn in the back garden, not far from the spot where yesterday Jeremy James had fallen off his tricycle. Timothy had come round to play, and although Jeremy James didn't really want to play with him, Mummy had said he should go and get some fresh air. Only he mustn't play any rough games like Cowboys and Indians because he had to be careful not to bump his wrist.

"A pained wrist never stopped *me* from playing Cowboys and Indians," said Timothy.

"Well, I had to have an egg-ray," said Jeremy James. "To see if my wrist was broken."

"It's not an egg-ray, it's an X-Ray. You don't know anything."

"Yes, I do, and I only had to have *one*, so it's an egg-ray."

Timothy pulled his six-shooter out of his holster and aimed it straight at Jeremy James's head.

"I've had lots of X-Rays, and I never cried once, and I played Cowboys and Indians straight after."

"I didn't cry," said Jeremy James. "Except just a bit."

"I'll bet you cried a lot," said Timothy. "Bang!"

A little puff of smoke came from the gun, as Timothy fired it.

"I only cried a tiny bit," said Jeremy James, "and I didn't cry at all in the hospital."

"Anybody can not cry in the hospital," said Timothy. "But I'll bet you cried buckets when you fell off your tricycle, and you should lie down dead 'cos I've just shot you."

Just then, Timothy's mother poked her head over the garden fence.

"Hello, darlings!" she cried. "Are you having a lovely game?"

"No," said Timothy.

"Oh, and what's poor Jeremy done to his little hand, then?"

Mrs Smyth-Fortescue never called him Jeremy James, and Jeremy James never called her Mrs Smyth-Fortescue.

"Hello, Mrs Might-Forceapoo," he said. "I've pained my wrist."

15

"Oh dear," said Mrs Smyth-Fortescue, "that must have been painful."

"No it wasn't," said Timothy. "But he cried all the same. I never cry when I pain my wrist, do I?"

"I don't think you've ever sprained your wrist, darling."

"Yes I have, lots of times."

"I don't think so, dear."

"Yes I have."

When they finished discussing whether Timothy had or had not sprained his wrist, Mrs Smyth-Fortescue announced that she was driving into town, and Timothy should come with her. A smile came to Jeremy James's face.

"No, I'll stay here and play with Jeremy James," announced Timothy, and the smile left Jeremy James's face.

"All right then, dear," said Mrs Smyth-Fortescue. "Since you're both getting along so well. Jeremy, just run and ask your Mummy if it'll be all right. Tell her I'll only be an hour or two."

"An hour or two!" cried Jeremy James. "But that's hours and hours!"

"Run along and ask your Mummy, dear."

Jeremy James ran along and asked his Mummy. He said, "Mummy, it won't be all right for Timothy to stay here for hours and hours, will it?"

But Mummy said it would. In fact, she said it twice, because Jeremy James asked her twice.

Fortunately, Daddy decided that he'd had enough

of thinking about planning to start trying to get down to doing some work, and came out into the garden with Jeremy James.

When Mrs Smyth-Fortescue had gone ("Dear Timothy won't be any trouble. The boys do get on so nicely, don't they?"), Daddy suggested a game of I-Spy.

"I-Spy's for little kids," said Timothy.

"Ah!" said Daddy. "Well, how about hide-and-seek?"

"Your garden's not big enough for hide-and-seek," said Timothy.

"Ah!" said Daddy. "How about blind man's buff?"

"Boring!" said Timothy.

"Hunt the thimble?"

"Boring!"

Daddy mentioned a game that Jeremy James had never heard of, called "Kill Your Neighbour", but Timothy wanted to play nothing except Cowboys and Indians.

"I'll be the cowboy," he said, "because I've got the gun, and you can be the Indians and I'll shoot you."

"What fun!" said Daddy. "No, I've got a better idea. We'll play football."

"I don't like football," said Timothy.

"Hold on, hold on," said Daddy. "Not ordinary football – too dangerous for Jeremy James. I'll be in goal, and you two can take it in turns to try and score."

"Boring," said Timothy.

"And whoever scores the most goals wins a bar of chocolate," said Daddy.

Timothy, who had just opened his mouth to say "boring", left his mouth open for a moment, and then murmured, "bar of chocolate". A bar of chocolate wasn't boring. A bar of chocolate was even worth playing football for.

"We'll play for twenty minutes," said Daddy.

'And I'll take the first kick," said Timothy.

"All right," said Daddy, "but that means Jeremy James takes the last kick."

Daddy fetched Jeremy James's football, and went and stood in front of the shed (at the side without a window). Then he rolled the ball gently towards Timothy.

Timothy's first shot missed the shed altogether and flew into the vegetable patch.

"Goal!" shouted Timothy.

"What do you mean, goal?" said Daddy. "You missed!"

"You didn't stop it," said Timothy, "so it's a goal."

Daddy explained that the ball had to hit the shed, and Timothy said it didn't. If the ball beat the goal-keeper, said Timothy, it was a goal, because those were the rules, and he knew because he'd seen real football on television, and that was how it was played.

"The ball goes into a net in real football," said Daddy. "But as we haven't got a net, we're going to

18

use the side of the shed, and this is our garden, and those are the rules in our garden."

"Well I didn't know that," grumbled Timothy, "and it's not fair, 'cos I would have kicked the ball at the shed if—"

"Right, start again," said Daddy.

Timothy ran up and gave the ball an almighty kick, but the ball went straight into Daddy's tummy. Daddy said "Ouf!" as he caught it, and then he rolled it towards Jeremy James.

Jeremy James didn't kick the ball nearly as hard as Timothy had done, but it also went straight towards Daddy. As Daddy bent down to stop it, though, he slipped, and somehow the ball managed to roll under his body and hit the shed.

"Goal!" shouted Jeremy James.

"That's not fair!" shouted Timothy. "You stopped *my* ball, and you let Jeremy James's ball hit the shed."

"Terrible mistake," said Daddy. "What a blunder. One nil to Jeremy James."

For his next kick, Timothy dribbled the ball up to within a couple of yards of the shed.

"Hold on, you can't do—" said Daddy, but before he could say what Timothy couldn't do, Timothy showed just what he could do. The ball crashed into the side of the shed like an exploding shell.

"One all," said Timothy.

"Hmmph," said Daddy. "Good shot, Timothy, but you're not allowed to come that close."

"Yes I am," said Timothy. "I can come as close as I like."

"Not in our garden," said Daddy again, and took several paces across the lawn before drawing a line with the heel of his shoe.

"You can't come beyond this line," he said. "Either of you."

"It's one all," said Timothy.

"All right," said Daddy. "One all."

"That's not fair," said Jeremy James. "If Timothy had a kick from that close, then I should have a kick too."

"True," said Daddy. "Just one."

And so Jeremy James came up to within a couple of yards of Daddy, and kicked the ball straight past him.

"Two one," shouted Jeremy James, and ran back waving his right arm to the sky.

From then on, the game got fiercer and fiercer. Daddy made some brilliant saves, especially from Timothy's thunderbolts, but he also made some awful mistakes. Once, when Timothy had actually drawn level, Daddy dived the wrong way to one of Jeremy James's shots, but another time, when Jeremy James was two goals ahead, he completely missed an easy one from Timothy. The score mounted up, and the minutes ticked away.

"Twelve eleven to Jeremy James," called Daddy, "and three minutes to go . . ."

The excitement was now almost too much to

21

bear. The thousands of spectators that weren't watching would have been on their feet cheering every shot and every save. Timothy's face was as red as a Rovers' jersey, and he was running to take his shots as if the World Cup itself were the prize.

And then came the most dramatic moment of the most dramatic game in the whole history of world football. With thirty seconds to go, and the score at thirteen twelve to Jeremy James, Daddy accidentally kicked the ball right across the garden into the flower bed next to the fence. Timothy's legs were a whirl of pink as he ran after it. Then suddenly, as his toe made contact with a raised paving slab, the whirl turned into a sprawling dive, and down went Timothy in an untidy heap on the garden path.

If the thousands of spectators who were not watching the football had been cheering now, they would not even have heard their own cheers, so loud did Timothy howl.

Daddy ran across the lawn, and Jeremy James followed.

"Where does it hurt?" asked Daddy.

"*Waaaah-woooo!*"

Jeremy James put his hands to his ears, as Timothy pointed deafeningly to his left leg.

Daddy very gently prised Timothy's hands away from the damaged leg, and uncovered a tiny graze from which came the thinnest trickle of blood.

"*Waaaaaah-woooooo!*"

"Is that it?" asked Daddy.

Timothy gave an ear-splitting nod.

"Well, we'll soon get that seen to," said Daddy, and he picked Timothy up in his arms and carried him towards the house.

Mummy had already opened the kitchen door, having noticed that the air outside had been suddenly ripped apart.

"What happened?" she asked.

"Our hero fell over," said Daddy, "and grazed his knee."

"*Waaaaaah-woooooo!*"

Mummy fetched some cotton wool and a bowl of water, and while Daddy sat Timothy on his knee, Mummy gently cleaned away the little blob of blood.

"*Waaaaaaaaah-wooooooooo!*"

When she had finished, Mummy stuck a little piece of plaster over the graze. Then slowly the storm subsided, the floods receded, and an uneasy calm settled over the kitchen, disturbed only by the occasional gurgling gulp.

"Are you all right now, Timothy?" asked Mummy. Timothy nodded.

"Such courage!" said Daddy. "See if you can stand up."

Very carefully, Timothy put his right leg down on the floor, and then even more carefully lowered his left leg. Finally he allowed his whole body to follow, and stood quite still between Mummy and Daddy.

"Can you walk?" asked Mummy.

Timothy very carefully placed his right foot in front of his left and took a step forwards.

"That's wonderful," said Daddy. "A wonderful step, Timothy. Can you do another one?"

Timothy did another one.

"Extraordinary talent," said Daddy.

All this time, Jeremy James had been watching in silence, waiting to ask a vital question. Now he could wait no longer.

"Daddy," he said.

"Yes, Jeremy James?" said Daddy.

"Can I have my bar of chocolate?"

The question had a remarkable effect on Timothy. Suddenly, he seemed to forget completely about the terrible injury that had threatened to end his footballing career.

"It's not your bar of chocolate," he said.

"Yes it is," said Jeremy James.

"We didn't finish the game," said Timothy.

"I'm afraid you did," said Daddy. "The final whistle blew while you were stroking the garden path with your knee."

"That's not fair," said Timothy. "I should have had another kick!"

But Daddy said it *was* fair, the twenty minutes had passed, Jeremy James had won thirteen twelve, and the referee's decision was final.

"You're not the referee," said Timothy, "you're the goalkeeper."

"But," said Daddy, "it's my garden."

With that he handed Jeremy James an unopened, silver-papered, blue-wrapped bar of fruit and nut.

"Now why don't you go outside," said Mummy, "and play a nice quiet game together till Timothy's mother gets home?"

Timothy limped out with a scowl, and Jeremy James walked out with a smile – and a bar of chocolate.

"It's not fair," said Timothy. "I should have won that chocolate."

"The only prize you should have won," said Jeremy James, slowly peeling the wrapper, "is a prize for crying."

"I wasn't crying," said Timothy, eyes fixed on the brown squares poking out of the silver paper. "I was just shouting a little."

"You cried so loud," said Jeremy James, snapping off a square and popping it in his mouth, "that I had to shut my ears."

"Ears can't be shut," said Timothy, "and can I have a bit?"

"No," said Jeremy James. "Because I won it, and because you said you didn't cry but you did."

Jeremy James broke off another square, and Timothy watched it disappear.

"If I say I did cry, will you give me a bit?" he asked.

Jeremy James thought for a moment.

"I'll give you a bit," he said, "if you say you cried a lot."

"Icralot," mumbled Timothy.

"Say it properly," said Jeremy James.

"I cried a lot," said Timothy.

By the time Timothy had said that he'd cried a lot, cried more than Jeremy James, cried like a baby, lost the football match, was a silly boy, and should have his bottom smacked, he and Jeremy James between them had finished the bar of chocolate. Jeremy James reckoned it was the best game he had ever played with Timothy.

"Hello, darlings!" said a familiar voice over the garden fence. "Mummy's back. Have you had a lovely time together?"

"Yes, thank you," said Jeremy James, at the same time as Timothy was saying "No."

"That's good!" said Mrs Smyth-Fortescue. "And

26

you're such good boys, I've brought you back a little present."

She held her hands out over the fence, and in each hand was a blue-wrapped, silver-papered bar of fruit and nut.

"One for each of you," she said.

It really had been a very enjoyable afternoon.

CHAPTER THREE

Gran

Richard was the roly-poly boy who lived round the corner at No. 24. He had shiny cheeks, and Jeremy James always liked playing with him, because he was nice and kind and fun and not Timothy.

The only problem in Richard's house was Gran. She was very old and tiny and sort of dry, and she sat in the armchair all day sleeping. The only time she didn't sleep was when Richard and Jeremy James wanted to play a game. If it was a video game, she'd be wanting to watch something on the TV, and if it was any other sort of game, she'd wait till they were right in the middle of it, and then she'd think of something for Richard to do. There was always something for Richard to do. Richard reckoned she just sat there all day thinking up new things for him to do, and if there weren't any new things, she'd ask him to do the old things.

"Richard, dear," she'd say, "would yer fetch me book/pen/pencil/newspaper/purse/slippers/cushion/pills/powders . . ."

Or: "Would yer just pop round to the store and

buy me some apples/bread/milk/sugar/salt/vinegar/mustard/envelopes/stamps/pills/powders . . ."

Gran had a lot of pills and powders. She ate pills and powders like some people eat chocolate.

"Richard, dear, would yer just come and put this plug in/pull that plug out/post this letter/find me glasses/open the curtain/ close the window/switch on the radio/switch off the telly . . ."

Once she'd sent Richard to the library, and Jeremy James had gone with him. They'd taken Richard's gerbil, which had escaped and caused a lot of people to scream and jump on tables. That wouldn't have happened if Gran hadn't said, "Richard, would yer just pop round to the library and change me books."

The trouble was, Gran's legs were very bad. She was always saying how bad her legs were. "Oooh me legs are bad today," she'd say, and that meant she couldn't get up and do anything. And *that* meant Richard had to get up and do something.

It wouldn't have been quite such a problem if Richard's mum and dad didn't both go to work, but as they were out most of the day, it was Gran who looked after Richard. And *that* meant Richard looked after Gran.

On this particular day, Richard wanted to show Jeremy James his new tree-house, which his dad had built for him.

"Just going into the garden, Gran, to play in the tree-house," said Richard.

"All right, dear," said Gran.

Then as Richard opened the French windows, Gran said: "Oh, Richard, dear, before yer go, could yer just fetch me walkin' stick. It's in the hall."

"Yes, Gran," said Richard, and slipped out into the hall.

Jeremy James's eyes had opened wide. He'd never seen a stick walking before, and he waited eagerly for it to come striding through the door. He was a bit disappointed when Richard came back carrying it.

"Is your stick going to walk, Gran?" he asked.

"My stick walk?" repeated Gran. "No, of course it isn't."

"Then why's it called a walking stick?" asked Jeremy James.

Richard told Jeremy James that the stick was just supposed to help Gran to walk.

"It's because me legs are bad," said Gran. "Ooooh they are bad, specially today. This is a very bad day for me legs. Richard, dear, just help me get up from here, will yer?"

With a lot of oohing and aahing, she heaved herself out of the chair, with Richard and Jeremy James pulling and pushing. Then she took the stick in her hand, and leaned on it.

It was the first time Jeremy James had ever seen Gran get out of the chair. He'd always thought she lived in it.

"Are you coming to the tree-house with us?" he asked.

"No, dear," said Gran. "Can't do the climbin'. It's me legs, yer see. Can't climb trees with me legs."

"Perhaps you could use your hands," said Jeremy James.

"Then what would I hold me stick with?" asked Gran.

Jeremy James watched as she took a couple of shaky steps across the room.

"Your stick isn't very good, is it?" said Jeremy James.

"Isn't it?" asked Gran.

"Not if it's supposed to help you walk," said Jeremy James. "I can walk a lot better than that *without* a stick."

31

"Ah yes," said Gran, "but then you haven't got my legs, have yer?"

Jeremy James wouldn't have wanted Gran's legs. He much preferred his own.

"Can we go now, Gran?" asked Richard.

"Yes, off yer go," said Gran.

But just as Richard and Jeremy James were heading again for the garden, she said: "Oh Richard, dear, before yer go, could yer just slip into the hall an' open the lavatory door for me. Yer know how it sticks."

"Ye-e-es, Gra-a-an," said Richard, and slipped out into the hall.

"If your Gran sits down on the lavatory," said Jeremy James, when Richard had come back, "she might never get up again."

"I know," said Richard. "I hope she doesn't ask me to help her up from *there*."

To get to the tree-house, they had to climb a wooden ladder. Richard climbed it very slowly and huffily-puffily, sounding a bit like Gran getting out of her chair. Jeremy James (whose wrist was quite better now) pretended he was a fireman, and blazed his way to the top. Once they were up there, it was exciting to look round at the branches and look up at the sky and look down at the grass. You could imagine you were a lion or a tiger resting there.

The house itself was a platform in the fork of the tree, and it was all fenced in so that you couldn't fall off. Richard had a waterproof box with some toys in

it, and toys in a tree were a lot more interesting than toys on the ground. A little racing car, for instance, went skidding across the platform, under the fence, and crashing down to the grass below. You couldn't do that on the ground. And fishing with a magnetic rod was six times more fun when the fish were six foot below than when they were just lying on the carpet. And when a brown speckled bird landed on a branch two feet away and dropped a splashy white splodge on to the lawn, the two boys simply howled with laughter.

"Why don't we have tea up here?" suggested Richard, two hours before tea-time.

"Good idea," said Jeremy James, who was ready for tea at any time.

Richard's Mum had left sandwiches and cakes for them in the kitchen, and so Jeremy James the fireman hot-footed it down the ladder. Richard then lowered himself hippopotamously, rung by rung.

"I hope Gran's asleep," whispered Richard. "Let's tiptoe through the living-room."

But Gran wasn't asleep. Gran wasn't in the living-room at all.

"That's funny," said Richard. "I wonder where she is."

They didn't have to wonder long.

"Richard!" came a muffled voice. "Richard, where are you?"

"I'm here, Gran," cried Richard. "Where are *you*?"

34

"I'm in the lavatory, dear! I can't get out."

Richard and Jeremy James hurried into the hall.

"The door's jammed," said Gran from inside the lavatory. "See if you can open it."

Richard tugged the handle, but the door didn't move. Jeremy James again tugged the handle, and again the door didn't move.

"You'll have ter get some help," said Gran. "Fetch the fire brigade."

Jeremy James didn't think the fire brigade would be much help, unless Gran was to start a fire in the lavatory. But it did give him an idea. He himself had once been locked in the bathroom, and Daddy had climbed up a ladder and crawled through the window to rescue him.

"Is there a window in the lavatory?" he asked Richard.

Richard said there was, and so the two boys went outside to have a look at it. There was quite a big square window which couldn't be opened, but above that was a little one which *was* open.

"We can climb through that and rescue Gran!" said Jeremy James.

"*I* can't climb through that!" said Richard. "I'd get stuck."

"Well I can," said Jeremy James.

"Where are yer?" cried Gran. "What yer doin'?"

"We're outside, Gran," said Jeremy James, "and we're going to rescue you."

"Fetch the fire brigade!" cried Gran.

Jeremy James remembered what Daddy had said to him when he'd been locked in.

"Keep calm, Gran," he said. "Nothing to worry about. We'll soon get you out of there."

"How are you going to climb up?" asked Richard.

"The tree-house ladder," said Jeremy James. "Come and help me carry it."

And so with a few more reassuring words to Gran, they went back into the house, through the living-room, out into the garden, and across to the tree-house. Then together, they tipped the ladder on to its side and, like a pair of hi-ho window-cleaners, marched back across the garden, round the side of the house, and up to the lavatory window. Then they stood the ladder on end, and Jeremy James climbed to the top and peeped through the open window. Gran was sitting on the lavatory.

"What yer doin'?" asked Gran looking up at Jeremy James looking down.

"What are *you* doing?" asked Jeremy James. He certainly didn't want to climb through the window if Gran was still doing what she'd gone to do in the first place.

"I'm sittin' here waitin' fer the fire brigade," said Gran.

"Have you finished doing your Number Two?" asked Jeremy James.

Gran said she'd been in there long enough to finish a hundred and fifty Number Twos, and – as Jeremy James poked his head, shoulders and arms through

36

the narrow gap – what did he think *he* was doing?

Jeremy James said he was coming in, and before Gran could even begin to heave herself off the lavatory seat, he'd come tumbling down over the window-sill, past the sink, and on to the floor at her feet.

"Ouch!" said Jeremy James. "Owowow!"

"Oooh!" said Gran. "Owowooooh!"

"I've hurt my wrist!" said Jeremy James.

"You've hurt me leg!" said Gran. "The bad one. The really bad one. Both me legs are bad, but you've hurt the really bad one."

Jeremy James picked himself up and felt his left wrist. It was painful. He could feel the pain climbing into his eyes, but he made it go down again. Heroes rescue Grans before they cry.

"What's happening?" called Richard from the foot of the ladder outside.

"It's all right," shouted Jeremy James.

And everything would have been all right if it hadn't been for one small detail that Jeremy James had not thought about before. Now that he'd got into the lavatory, how were he and Gran going to get out?

He pushed the door, but it wouldn't open. Then he hit it with his right hand, rammed it with his right foot, shoved it with his shoulder, knocked it with his knee, hammered it with his hip, and banged it with his bottom. But still the door wouldn't open.

"Richard!" called Gran.

"Yes, Gran?" called Richard.

"Go an' see if there's anyone next door!"

"All right, Gran."

There was a long silence. Gran sat on the seat, holding her walking stick, and Jeremy James stood at the door holding his wrist.

"Are you there, Gran?" came Richard's voice eventually.

"Course I'm here!" said Gran. "Well?"

"There *is* somebody next door," said Richard. "I saw Mr Biddle in his living-room. He's watching cricket on TV."

"Is he comin'?" asked Gran.

"No," said Richard.

"Why not?" asked Gran.

"'Cos he's in his living-room," said Richard.

"Did yer tell him we were stuck in here?" asked Gran.

"No," said Richard. "You just told me to see if anyone was there."

Gran groaned and told Richard to fetch Mr Biddle. A few minutes later Mr Biddle arrived, pulled open the lavatory door ("Ah, it's the spinkle-hasket-toggle-brock!") and Gran and Jeremy James came out into the hall.

"Are you all right, Gran?" asked Mr Biddle.

"Yes, thanks very much, Mr Biddle," said Gran. "I'm all right. It's just me legs, yer know."

"Are you all right, Jeremy James?" asked Richard.

But Jeremy James was not all right. His wrist hurt. A lot.

"I think I've pained it," he said with a screwed-up voice.

Mr Biddle hurried back to his living-room ("England need me," he said), Gran went to the kitchen to make herself a cup of tea, and Jeremy James went home to have his wrist seen to. The last thing he heard as he left Richard's house was the voice of Gran:

"Richard, dear, would yer just get me some milk."

CHAPTER FOUR

The Parcel

Daddy had gone into town, and everybody else was relaxing in the garden. Mummy and the twins were asleep in the shade of the apple tree, and Jeremy James was thinking that it was time for some chocolate.

The more Jeremy James thought about his chocolate, the more he needed it. His mouth ached for the bite-chew-yumminess of the fruit and nut bar he had put on the top shelf of the fridge. It seemed to be calling him. "Come and get me!" it was saying. "I'm so lonely in here! Jeremy James! Jeremy James! Come and eat me!"

Jeremy James could ignore the call no longer. Taking care not to disturb Mummy, he padded across the lawn and into the kitchen. There he opened the fridge door, and took out the blue-wrapped bar of heavenly delight. He held it tenderly in his bandaged left hand, and with his expert chocolate-breaking right hand was just about to peel and snap when . . .

DING-DONG!

That was the front doorbell. Jeremy James was so

surprised that he dropped the chocolate on the floor. The DING-DONG had sounded almost like CAUGHT YOU, although it was *his* chocolate, and he wasn't doing anything naughty.

He picked up the bar, put it back in the fridge, and hurried to the front door. And there stood a small round-shaped postman carrying a large square-shaped packet.

"Parcel for you," he said. "Can you manage? It's a bit heavy."

Jeremy James took the parcel. It *was* heavy, but he held it tightly against his chest.

"Yes, thank you," he said.

The postman closed the front door for him, and he carried the parcel into the living-room, where he managed to lift it up on to the table. Then he climbed on to a chair, and had a good look. (For some reason the chocolate had now stopped calling.)

It was an interesting parcel. It was box-like, wrapped in brown paper, tied up with string, and had various labels on it, including some red ones. These contained one word, but although he could read the letters – F-R-A-G-I-L-E – he didn't know the word they spelt.

Now a box like that could hold any number of things. A hundred bars of chocolate to start with. Or maybe toys. Or books. Or clothes. Chocolate and sweets would be best. Clothes would be worst.

Jeremy James grasped the parcel in both hands and shook it. There was just a slight rattle, but it wasn't a sound you could definitely say belonged to chocolate, toys or books. On the other hand, clothes wouldn't make any sort of rattle, because clothes were soft. Good.

A parcel like that really needed to be opened quickly. If it *was* chocolate, it could easily melt. Now that would be – as Daddy said once when his football team lost in the last minute – a tragedy.

Jeremy James climbed down from the chair, and ran out into the garden to the apple tree. Mummy was still fast asleep.

"Jem Jem!" said Jennifer, climbing to her feet in the play-pen, and smiling broadly. "Play with Jeffer?"

"I'm busy," said Jeremy James. "There's a parcel. A very important parcel."

He looked at Mummy, hoping she'd heard, but she hadn't.

"Parcel!" said Jennifer. "Portant parcel."

"It's got to be opened," said Jeremy James. "Before it melts."

But still Mummy remained stubbornly asleep.

"Melts!" said Jennifer. "Choc-let." (Like her elder brother, Jennifer was an expert on this subject.)

"That's right!" said Jeremy James.

Christopher now scrambled to his feet.

"Choc-let!" he cried. "Where?"

"It's in the parcel!" said Jeremy James.

"Here!" cried Jennifer. "Choc-let here!"

Jeremy James again looked at Mummy, but despite the excitement and the urgency of her children's needs, she was still unwakably asleep.

"It might not be chocolate," said Jeremy James. "It could be toys, or books, or clothes."

"Choc-let!" said Jennifer.

"Choc-let!" said Christopher.

It just had to be chocolate, since everybody wanted it to be chocolate, but how long would it stay chocolate? If it wasn't opened soon, it would turn into brown liquid, and then it would start dripping through the paper all over the table, all over the living-room, all over the house. The house would be flooded. Mind you, a house flooded with chocolate could be fun ... But Mummy and Daddy wouldn't like it, would they? They'd say, "Jeremy James, why didn't you open the parcel and put the chocolate in the fridge, before it melted?" He could hear them saying it.

Jeremy James went back into the house, and climbed on to the chair again. Then he picked up the parcel and examined it for dripping brown stains. There were none, but again the box gave a little rattle. Maybe it was sweets after all. But sweets could melt too. Anything could melt in this heat.

Jeremy James climbed down and went into the kitchen. He picked up the scissors from the kitchen table, and returned to the living-room. With two big snips he cut the string, and then with a few more snips and rips he removed all the brown paper, revealing a cardboard box which was sealed with brown tape. Snip, rip, and away came the brown tape, and the box was ready for opening.

Jeremy James lifted the lid, and found that the box was full of soft paper. It wasn't chocolate-wrapping paper. It wasn't even sweet-wrapping paper. It was nothing-wrapping paper. He took it out, and put it on the table. Ah! There was something in the middle of the box – something hard, though it was wrapped in something soft. The something soft was a sort of bubbly material. Jeremy James lifted the whole thing out of the box, which he pushed aside with his elbow, and set it down on the table in front of him.

It certainly wasn't chocolate. Or sweets, or toys, or books, or clothes. It was something solid, and it wasn't melting, and there was just one of it, and it was heavy, and it was a funny shape, and it rattled a bit. So what was it?

There was only one way to find out. Mummy and Daddy would still be pleased with him if he had saved them the trouble of undoing the parcel, opening the box, and taking all the wrapping paper out. That was a lot of work, and Mummy and Daddy were always saying what a lot of work they had. Well, they wouldn't have to do this work. Jeremy James was doing it for them.

With a few more snips, he cut away the bubbly material, and came to a piece of gold-coloured metal. The metal was loosely attached to some glass, and as the rest of the bubbly material fell away, there lay the mystery object: a sort of pear-shaped lump of glass with a rattly piece of metal on it. Anything more unchocolate, unsweet, untoy, unbook, or even unclothing it was hard to imagine.

"What is it?" Jeremy James asked himself aloud.

Maybe the other side might be more interesting. Jeremy James picked it up to see.

And then something terrible happened. In order to do all the work that Mummy and Daddy now wouldn't have to do, Jeremy James had stood on the chair beside the table. But as he picked up the strange lump of glass, the chair seemed to slip away from him, and Jeremy James slipped with it, and the strange lump of glass slipped with Jeremy James, and all of them – chair, Jeremy James, and lump of glass – went crashing down to the floor below.

"Ouch!" cried Jeremy James. "Owowow!"

"Thump!" went the chair.

And "Crash-tinkle-splinter!" went the lump of glass.

Jeremy James lay on the floor, wondering which parts of his body were going to start hurting. One of them in particular was quick to send him a message: it was the one with a bandage on it.

"Owowow!" said Jeremy James again.

"What's happened? Oh good heavens, what's all this glass?"

Mummy, startled out of her sleep by what sounded like a bomb in the living-room, had come rushing in from the garden.

"Jeremy James, are you all right? Where did all this glass come from?"

Jeremy James thought of explaining to Mummy about the melting chocolate and the house being flooded, but he had a feeling that a few tears might be more use to him at the moment than a few words of explanation. Besides, his wrist really did hurt. It hurt enough for him to cry real tears.

When Daddy came home from town, he found the whole family out in the garden under the apple tree. Mummy was reading, Jeremy James looked as if he'd been crying, and the twins were playing quietly in their play-pen.

"Dad-dy!" cried Jennifer as he crossed the lawn.

Daddy bent down to kiss Mummy.

"Jem-Jem nor-ty!" said Jennifer.

"What's that?" asked Daddy.

Mummy explained that Jeremy James had opened a parcel containing the beautiful and very expensive lamp that she and Daddy had ordered from the beautiful and very expensive lamp shop in Castlebury two weeks ago.

"Ah!" said Daddy. "I was wondering when that would come."

"It came this afternoon," said Mummy.

"Good," said Daddy.

"It also went this afternoon," said Mummy.

"What do you mean?" asked Daddy.

"You'd better ask Jeremy James," said Mummy.

Daddy did ask Jeremy James. And Jeremy James explained, through a new trickle of tears, all about melting chocolate, and the house being flooded, and saving Mummy and Daddy lots of work, and . . .

"You dropped it," said Daddy.

"Yes," said Jeremy James.

He also told Daddy how he'd pained his wrist again, and Daddy said that maybe he ought to pain Jeremy James's bottom.

"You shouldn't go opening parcels, should you?" he said.

Jeremy James agreed.

"You could have had a really nasty accident, and fallen on some broken glass."

Jeremy James agreed.

"And even if it had been chocolate, it wouldn't have been *your* chocolate, would it?"

Jeremy James agreed.

"Let that be a lesson to you. No more parcel opening, right?"

Jeremy James agreed.

Then Mummy said maybe they should all go in and have some tea, and everyone agreed.

Two weeks later, Jeremy James happened to be playing with his racing cars when the postman rang. It was another heavy parcel, just like the first one. Jeremy James got the postman to put it down, and he went and told Daddy, who was in his study.

"It's a heavy parcel, like the first one!" said Jeremy James, and followed Daddy into the hall.

"It is indeed," said Daddy, picking it up. "But this time we shall make light of it."

Carefully Daddy carried the parcel into the living-room, and put it on the table.

"Now then, Jeremy James," he said, "let's show you how to open a parcel."

He snipped the string, snip-ripped the brown paper and the parcel tape, and opened the box. Then he took out all the wrapping paper, removed the bubbly material, and triumphantly lifted up the beautiful and very expensive glass lamp.

"And that, Jeremy James," he said, "is how you open a parcel without breaking the contents."

As he said it, he turned away from the table, and his right foot landed on Jeremy James's blue racing car. The car and the foot both skidded forwards, while the rest of Daddy seemed to go backwards, and the next moment his bottom hit the living-room carpet with a dull thump. Meanwhile, the lamp had jumped high in the air, and fallen to the floor with a loud and shattering and all-too-familiar crash.

After that, Mummy and Daddy decided it would be best to keep the old lamp for the time being. And Jeremy James agreed.

CHAPTER FIVE

Chocolate

"You're eating far too many sweets," said Mummy. "It's sweets and chocolate and cakes and ice cream all day long."

"I don't think it's too many," said Jeremy James. "I could eat a lot more."

"It's *far* too many," said Mummy. "And you've even got the twins at it now."

"Choc-let!" said Jennifer in her high chair, speaking through a mouthful of banana.

"Choc-let!" said Christopher, losing a mouthful of banana from his high chair.

"There you are!" said Mummy. "Choc-let! Choc-let! Nothing but choc-let."

"Yes, please," said Jennifer.

The family were at the table, and just because Jeremy James hadn't been hungry for vegetable lasagne, Mummy had started to talk about sweets. It was true that Jeremy James had had a few sweets this morning, and a couple of squares of chocolate. Well, half a bar, actually, but it was only the half bar left over from the bar he'd started the previous night, and you should never leave things once you've started them. But that wasn't the reason for his not being hungry for vegetable lasagne. He didn't like vegetable lasagne. Or at least he didn't like vegetable lasagne as much as he liked chocolate.

"At this rate," said Mummy, "you'll have no teeth by the time you're twenty."

Jeremy James frowned.

"Why won't I have any teeth?" he asked.

"They'll have rotted away," said Mummy. "Remember what Mr Pulham told you about the Tooth-Dragon?"

Mr Pulham was the dentist who'd killed a Tooth-Dragon in Jeremy James's mouth.

"Tooth-Dragons like sweet things," said Mummy. "That's what he told you."

"But Daddy eats chocolate," said Jeremy James.

"Choc-let!" said Jennifer.

"Choc-let!" said Christopher.

"Daddy doesn't eat as much as you," said Mummy. "And anyway, Daddy's giving it up."

Jeremy James looked wide-eyed at Daddy, and Daddy looked down at the table-cloth and nodded, a little sadly.

"It's true," he said. "The supreme sacrifice. No more chocolate."

"Choc-let!" cried Jennifer.

"Choc-let!" cried Christopher.

"What about sweets?" asked Jeremy James.

"Sweets!" cried Jennifer.

"Sweets!" cried Christopher.

"Sweets as well," said Daddy. "From now on, Jeremy James, we're going to eat nothing but healthy things like fresh fruit and vegetables. Then we'll both grow up to be big and strong. Like your mother."

Mummy laughed, but Jeremy James didn't think it was funny. Fruit and vegetables instead of sweets and chocolate was no joke. It was the same old story. Whatever you liked was bad for you, and you had to eat/drink/do what you didn't like to be a good boy. Did a grown-up ever ask you to give up vegetable lasagne? Or cabbage, or tomatoes, or oranges?

"Now finish your lasagne," said Mummy.

Jeremy James chewed the mouthful of lasagne that he'd been chewing since Mummy first mentioned chocolate. It was like chewing rubber.

"Why is rubber good for you and chocolate bad for you?" asked Jeremy James.

"What?" said Mummy.

"Bacteria," said Daddy.

Daddy always used long words when you asked him a difficult question. Mummy usually said "Hmmph", and Daddy usually said "Worple, worple semantics", but this time Daddy said "Bacteria".

"They're little tiny weeny creatures," said Daddy, "that love sugar. So if you get sugar on your teeth, they come along and eat your teeth. Or something like that."

"Well, if I kept my mouth closed," said Jeremy James, "they wouldn't be able to get in, would they?"

"If you kept your mouth closed," said Daddy, "the chocolate wouldn't be able to get in either."

"Choc-let!" squealed Jennifer.

"Choc-let!" squealed Christopher.

"I could put the chocolate in very quickly," said Jeremy James.

"Not quickly enough," said Daddy. "Besides, for all you know, the bacteria could be *in* the chocolate."

Jeremy James thought for a moment.

"If they're in the chocolate," he said, "why haven't they eaten it themselves?"

"It's all a matter of worple worple semantics," said Daddy.

Jeremy James reckoned it was all a matter of grown-ups not knowing what was good for little boys. And when afters turned out to be fresh fruit salad *without ice cream*, he knew that this would never again be home, sweet home.

During the weeks that followed, the family ate nothing but "healthy" food. That meant fruit, vegetables, fish, vegetables, fruit, salad, fruit, vegetables, wholemeal bread, vegetables, fruit, plain yoghurt, and fruit and vegetables.

One day Mummy announced that she had lost ten pounds. Jeremy James immediately offered to find it for her, but it turned out she meant weight and not money, and she was pleased with herself.

"It's all done by eating the right things," she said.

"Have I lost weight too, Mummy?" asked Jeremy James.

"I hope not," said Mummy. "We don't want *you* to get thinner."

"I *am* getting thinner," said Jeremy James, "so maybe I should eat some wrong things, and . . ."

But Mummy soon proved that Jeremy James was not getting thinner. She made him stand on the bathroom scales, and he was two pounds heavier than when he'd last stood on them. For some reason, this proved that healthy food was good for Mummy, because she lost weight, and good for Jeremy James because he gained weight. Jeremy James did suggest that maybe he'd gain even more weight if he ate wrong things, but Mummy just said "Hmmph" and they went downstairs again.

Two days later, Jeremy James developed a sore throat. It was only slightly sore, but Mummy had a look and thought the throat was rather red, so she made an appointment for Jeremy James to see Dr Bassett.

"I'll take him," said Daddy. "I could do with an outing. Might freshen me up a bit."

Jeremy James had seen Dr Bassett before, when he'd been taken ill with liquorice allsorts flu. Dr Bassett was the tallest man in the world, and even when he sat down, he was tall enough to be standing up.

"Hello, John. Hello, Jeremy James," he said, when they entered the surgery. "Don't tell me. Let me guess. It's allsortitis."

"Well no, it's not actually," said Daddy. "He's got a bit of a sore throat."

"Ah!" said Dr Bassett. "Swallowed the packet as well, did he? Come here, Jeremy James, and let's have a look."

He got Jeremy James to open his mouth, and then he shone a little torch inside.

"Well now, old chap," he said, "what you've got there is a touch of tonsillitis. Bit of inflammation. Nothing serious. I'll give you some antibiotics."

Jeremy James didn't know what tonsillitis or inflammation were, but he knew what he hoped antibiotics were.

"Are they like liquorice allsorts?" he asked.

"What?" asked Dr Bassett.

"Antibottics," said Jeremy James.

"Afraid not," said Dr Bassett. "They're just pills to make your throat better. You've got some bacteria in there, so we'll try to kill them off. Right?"

Jeremy James's eyes opened wide.

"Bacteria?" he cried.

Dr Bassett looked surprised. "You know what they are?" he asked.

"They're tiny things that like sugar," said Jeremy James.

"Clever lad!" said Dr Bassett.

"But I haven't had any sugar," said Jeremy James. "Because I haven't had any sweets. I've only had fruit and vegibles and fish and yoghurt and brown bread."

Dr Bassett explained that bacteria were all over the place, and not just in sugar. Jeremy James asked if they were in vegetable lasagne.

"Could be," said Dr Bassett. "Who knows where the little devils hide themselves!"

Jeremy James found this very interesting, and he would have liked to ask some more questions. But what happened next was even more interesting. What happened next was the most interesting thing to have happened in all the weeks of sweetlessness.

Dr Bassett began to write on a piece of paper, and as he did so, he asked Daddy how *he* was.

"I'm fine, Robert, thanks," said Daddy. "Except that I seem to get very tired these days."

"So do I, John," said Dr Bassett. "So do I. Especially in the afternoons. Find myself nodding off in the middle of a diagnosis. You know what I do?"

Daddy shook his head. Dr Bassett reached out and opened a drawer, from which – with a little flourish of his hand – he produced... a bar of chocolate.

"A few squares of this," he said, "and I can write ten prescriptions a minute."

"Chocolate!" cried Jeremy James.

Jennifer and Christopher would also have cried "Choc-let!" if they'd been there.

"Just ups the blood-sugar," said Dr Bassett. "Here, have a piece."

Daddy and Jeremy James each took the piece that was offered to them, and as their lips closed and their teeth sank into the firm square of taste-bud-tingling delight, a look of exquisite pleasure spread across their faces.

"Mmmm!" said Daddy.

"Mmmm!" said Jeremy James.

"It's just ordinary chocolate," said Dr Bassett.

"It may be ordinary to you," said Daddy, "but it's a feast for us, eh, Jeremy James?"

"Mmmm!" said Jeremy James.

There was a long family discussion that evening. Jeremy James told Mummy all about the bacteria, Daddy told Mummy all about blood-sugar, and Mummy told Daddy and Jeremy James all about healthy food (again).

"What's needed here," said Daddy, "is compromise."

"What's needed here," said Jeremy James, "is chocolate."

"Choc-let!" said Jennifer.

"Choc-let!" said Christopher.

It turned out, though, that by "compromise" Daddy actually meant chocolate. And sweets and ice cream and cakes. But not too many. That was the important thing. They could be eaten in small quantities, and Jeremy James must ask Mummy first. Daddy didn't have to ask Mummy first, and Mummy didn't have to ask anybody because she wasn't going to eat sweet things anyway. And the twins would only have what Mummy gave them. Daddy said that was fair, Jeremy James said that was fairly fair, and the twins said "Choc-let!"

The next day, Mummy announced a special treat for lunch. She brought in a cheese and broccoli quiche. Jeremy James (whose sore throat was now better) had hoped it might be chicken and chips, but Mummy didn't cook chips any more. Not healthy, she said. The quiche was nice, especially for someone who hadn't had a thing to eat since breakfast, but it was hardly a special treat.

"The special treat," said Mummy, "is for dessert."

And dessert turned out to be fresh fruit salad, *with ice cream*. Jeremy James enjoyed his second helping as much as his first, and even Mummy had a spoonful and said how nice it was.

"I'd forgotten how nice ice cream can be!" said Mummy.

"I hadn't!" said Jeremy James.

All the same, he was not allowed a third helping, and later that afternoon he was not allowed to eat any chocolate. At least, not until he happened to find Daddy munching a piece in the kitchen. Daddy explained that he was feeling a bit tired, and was just upping his blood-sugar.

"I'm tired, too," said Jeremy James.

Daddy grinned, broke off a square, and he and Jeremy James untired themselves together.

CHAPTER SIX

The Fortune-Teller

There was a funfair on Cannon Green. Daddy said he thought Jeremy James would enjoy that. Mummy said she thought Daddy would enjoy it, too.

"Roundabouts, dodgem-cars, games, prizes," said Daddy. "Just the thing for little boys."

"Not to mention big boys," said Mummy.

And so Daddy and Jeremy James drove to Cannon Green, parked the car, and made their way towards the blaring music, the flashing lights, and the huge turning wheel that you could see even from the car-park.

The fun actually started before you got to Cannon Green, because along the path were stalls selling sweets, chocolate, ice cream, candy floss, and all the things that used to be good until they became bad. Jeremy James had a huge whirl of pink candy floss, but Daddy gritted his teeth and stopped himself from buying a bar of chocolate. Then he ungritted his teeth, and bought one.

"It's a treat," he said.

The whole funfair was a treat. Jeremy James drove

a car on a roundabout, while Daddy sat beside him and got dizzy. Then Daddy drove a car on the dodgems, while Jeremy James sat beside him and got bumped. A long-haired young man with a short-haired girlfriend drove into them and laughed, but Daddy managed to bump them back, and then Daddy laughed.

Jeremy James won a paintbox when he chose a special ticket, and Daddy won nothing when he fired a gun at some tin soldiers and missed. Then they both went on the Giant Slide, and they would also have gone on the Big Wheel if Daddy hadn't said that big wheels were just roundabouts turned on their side, and roundabouts made him go green.

Instead, Daddy tried to win a Red Indian kit for Jeremy James by throwing darts at some playing cards. Unfortunately, he missed as many cards with the darts as he'd missed soldiers with the gun.

"If you was a Red Indian throwin' tomahawks," said the man in the booth, "they'd 'ave to evacuate the camp."

There were so many things to see, and so many things to do, and so many people and so much noise that Jeremy James's head was buzzing. He didn't mind the buzz, though, because it was exciting, but Daddy must have had a less exciting buzz, because he wanted to find somewhere a bit quieter.

"All this oompah-crash-taraa-ra-ra is giving me a headache," he shouted.

"Is that why you missed with the darts, Daddy?" shouted Jeremy James.

"Well ... hmmph ... hum ... worple worple," said Daddy.

They made their way towards a corner of Cannon Green where there seemed to be fewer people and less taraa-ra-ra, and it was there that Daddy spotted a caravan with a notice outside: MADAME CLARE VOYANT, FORTUNE-TELLER. Underneath these words was a picture of a very beautiful gypsy girl.

"Would you like to have your fortune told?" asked Daddy.

"Does that mean she'll tell me how much money I've got?" asked Jeremy James.

"No," said Daddy, "it means she'll tell you your future."

It seemed to Jeremy James that if his future was connected to a fortune, it would certainly be a good idea to see the gypsy. And so he and Daddy climbed the two steps, and stood before the open red curtain, peering into the darkness.

"Come in, me dears," said a cracked old voice, and in they went.

On the other side of the curtain sat a little old lady dressed in colourful gypsy clothes.

"We've come to see Madame Clare Voyant," said Daddy.

"Then yer've come ter the right place," said the lady. "Forchunes fer both of yer?"

"Yes, please."

"That'll be three pounds, then, dearie."

"Hm, forchunes for you too," said Daddy. "Isn't it half price for children?"

"No, it ain't," said the lady. "Children oughter be double price, 'cos they've got twice as much future."

"That's true," said Daddy, and then paid three pounds.

"This way then," said the old lady, closing the red curtain, and she led them at a hobble into the depths of the caravan.

There were curtains over all the windows, but in the dim light Jeremy James could see a lot of masks, plants, and ornaments on the walls. There was also a strange smell, as if something sweet was burning.

The noise from outside seemed a long way away now, and the new quietness was somehow heavy. It wasn't frightening, but it wasn't pleasant either. He was glad that he had hold of Daddy's hand.

The old lady led them to a table with a glass ball and some cards on it.

"Shoo!" she said, and a black cat jumped off the chair behind the table, then disappeared into the shadows.

"Now then," said the old lady, sitting down in its place, "which of yer's goin' ter be first?"

"Just a minute," said Daddy, as he and Jeremy James sat on the two chairs facing her. "We want to see Madame Clare Voyant."

"You *are* seein' 'er," said the old lady.

"You're not the lady in the picture!" said Jeremy James.

"Oh yes I am," said the old lady. "That's what the future c'n do to yer."

"Hmmph!" said Daddy. "Well, don't you think you ought to change the photo?"

"Whatchoo come for?" asked the old lady. "Ter see a pretty face or 'ave yer forchune told? 'Oo's first, then?"

"Jeremy James," said Daddy.

"Crystal, cards or 'and?"

Jeremy James looked at Daddy.

"Do you want the lady to see your future in the glass, in the cards, or in your hand?" asked Daddy.

Since Jeremy James couldn't see much future in

his hand or in the cards, he chose the glass ball.

Madame Clare then made some airy movements with her hand over the ball, and mumbled some words that sounded very like "Worple, worple semantics . . ."

"Aha!" she said. "Ah! Aha! Yes, right, hmmm . . . I see a fine young man, tall, good-lookin'."

"Where?" asked Jeremy James.

"In me crystal ball," answered Madame Clare.

Jeremy James stood up to have a closer look.

"I can't see anyone," he said.

"That's cos you 'aven't got the power," said Madame Clare. "You 'ave to 'ave special powers ter see inter the future. Now, this tall an' 'andsome young man . . . 'e's got an unusual name . . . Jem . . . Jemmy . . ."

"Jeremy James," said Jeremy James.

"Is that you? Well, I never! Special powers, see? 'Ow did I know your name?"

"Daddy said it."

"Oh! Well, I'm sure I never 'eard. Now stop interruptin'."

Once again Madame Clare passed her hands over the crystal ball, screwed up her wrinkles in a frown of concentration, and gazed intently into the future.

"You're goin' ter be very tall, an' very 'andsome."

"Will I be taller than Timothy?" asked Jeremy James.

"'Oo's Timofy?"

"The boy next door."

68

"Oh, you mean the Timofy next door. Yes, 'e's short compared ter you. Ugly. Dark 'air . . ."

"Timothy's got red hair."

"That's right, dark red. But I'm lookin' at you now. An' I see a big 'ouse wiv a big garden . . ."

"We've only got a small house with a small garden," said Jeremy James. "You must be looking at Timothy's house."

"It's your *future* 'ouse, my dear," said Madame Clare.

Jeremy James looked into the crystal ball like a boy looking for a missing liquorice allsort, but still he could see nothing.

"I see you writin'," said Madame Clare. "Yes . . . letters, exams, cheques, books . . ."

"Daddy writes books," said Jeremy James.

"Does 'e?" said Madame Clare. "Well, that's it, then. You're goin' ter write books an' be rich an' famous."

Jeremy James smiled up at Daddy, and Daddy smiled down at Jeremy James. Next, Madame Clare announced that according to the latest crystal news bulletin, Jeremy James would have a beautiful fair-haired wife and five beautiful children – three boys and two girls – and would live till the ripe old age of 85.

"An' if this don't 'appen like I say, Jeremy James, yer can come back 'ere 'an I'll give you yer money back."

It was now Daddy's turn, and he told Madame

69

Clare to read his future in his hand. She very quickly discovered that he was an author, and lived with his family in a small house with a small garden.

"Let's see now," she said, "other children . . . I'm tryin' ter see if you've got other children."

"Christopher and Jennifer!" said Jeremy James.

"That's right," said Madame Clare. "A boy and a girl. They're older than Jeremy James . . ."

"No they're not!" said Jeremy James.

"Younger, I mean," said Madame Clare. "An' Jeremy James is older than them. Is that right?"

"Yes," said Jeremy James.

Then Madame Clare went on to talk about Daddy's books, and a possible move, and success, and to beware of a man with glasses who had something to do with money ("Is he a bank manager?" asked Daddy), and . . .

Jeremy James had now stopped listening to Madame Clare and to Daddy's future. His attention had been caught by a movement in the shadows behind the old lady. Something dark and slinky was easing its way along the shelf above her head. It was the black cat.

Madame Clare looked at Daddy's upraised palm, Daddy looked at Madame Clare, Jeremy James looked at the black cat, and the black cat looked at the large, dragon-painted vase right in the middle of the shelf beneath which Madame Clare was sitting.

"Excuse me!" said Jeremy James.

"Ssh!" said Madame Clare. "I see somethin' unexpected . . ."

"But the—"

"Somethin' very valu'ble . . ."

"The cat—"

"An' it's comin' your way . . ."

At precisely that moment, the black cat brushed against the large, dragon-painted vase, which tilted, toppled, and fell down with a loud *bonk* straight on to Madame Clare's head. The *bonk* was followed by three different noises: one was a miaowling screech from the cat, the second was a howling scream from Madame Clare, and the third was a clattering crash as the vase fell to the floor.

"Me head!" cried Madame Clare. "An' me vase!"

"And me future," murmured Daddy.

Fortunately, Madame Clare wasn't badly hurt, but her vase, her precious, been-in-the-family-for-generations Chinese-or-was-it-Japanese vase, would never be a vase again. It lay in at least twenty-two and a half pieces on the floor at her feet.

"Didn't you know it was going to fall?" asked Jeremy James.

"'Ow would I know that?" asked Madame Clare.

"I thought you knew the future," said Jeremy James.

Madame Clare rubbed her head.

"Nobody could 'ave known *that* sort of future," she said.

"*I* did," said Jeremy James.

71

Soon afterwards, when Daddy had made quite sure that Madame Clare was all right, he and Jeremy James left the caravan, walked back through the hustling-bustling hurly-burly, and drove home.

That evening, Jeremy James could talk of nothing else but the fortune-teller, the crystal ball, the black cat, and the vase.

"She didn't know it was going to fall," he told Mummy. "But I did."

There was one important question that Jeremy James still wanted to know the answer to, and so when Mummy and Daddy tucked him up in bed, he asked it.

"Am I really going to write books and be rich and famous?"

"Well," said Daddy. "If you don't become famous through writing books, maybe you'll make your fortune as a fortune-teller."

Jeremy James was still thinking about that when, without his even knowing it, let alone predicting it, he fell asleep.

CHAPTER SEVEN

Heaven

The gerbils were dead. Daddy had bought them on the twins' first birthday, and so Jeremy James had christened them Wiffer and Jeffer. He'd loved to hold them, and to watch them chasing round their cage, burrowing in the sawdust, or treadling their wheel. But last night they had both been lying quietly, and this morning they were lying dead.

"What made them die?" asked Jeremy James through his tears.

"Difficult to say without a post-mortem," answered Daddy.

"Will the postman bring one?" asked Jeremy James.

"A post-mortem's an examination," said Daddy, "to find the cause of death."

Jeremy James didn't want to examine Wiffer and Jeffer. He didn't even want to look at them lying there so still and stiff in the corner of their cage.

There had been a death in the family before. Great-Great-Aunt Maud had died at the age of ninety-two, and Jeremy James had gone to her funeral. She had been put in a beautiful shiny box, which Jeremy James would have liked to keep his toys and sweets in. Only the grown-ups had wasted it by putting it in the ground and covering it up with earth.

"We'll just bury them, shall we?" said Daddy. "Somewhere nice in the garden."

"Will we put them in a box?" asked Jeremy James. "Like Great-Great-Aunt Maud?"

"Yes," said Daddy. "Maybe you can go and find one, while I get things ready."

Jeremy James remembered something else about Great-Great-Aunt Maud.

"Can we have a party afterwards as well?" he asked.

"I expect Mummy will let us have a few sandwiches and cakes," said Daddy.

It so happened that Mummy had already planned to make sandwiches and cakes, because the Reverend Cole was coming round to discuss the church fête.

"Maybe if you ask him nicely," said Mummy, "the Reverend Cole might give the gerbils a proper burial."

Jeremy James thought that was a good idea, and so off he went to look for a box, while Mummy made the sandwiches and cakes, and Daddy went out into the garden to dig a grave.

The box that Jeremy James chose was bright and cheerful. Great-Great-Aunt Maud had been buried in one that was heavy and shiny and dark, but she'd been very old, and so maybe she hadn't liked cheerful boxes. The gerbils would have one that was covered in different-coloured blobs, each of which was a pleasure to look at whether you were alive or dead. It was an empty liquorice allsort box.

The Reverend Cole was very old, too, though not as old or as dead as Great-Great-Aunt Maud. He walked with a hobble, and talked with a wobble, and he had accidentally dropped Christopher in the font during the twins' christening. Jeremy James remembered that day very well, because he had accidentally been the cause of the Reverend Cole accidentally dropping Christopher.

"Never heard of dead marbles," said the Reverend Cole.

"Not marbles," said Jeremy James. "Gerbils."

"Ah!" said the Reverend Cole. "Where are they, then?"

"Here," said Jeremy James, holding out the liquorice allsort box.

"Thank you," said the Reverend Cole. "My favourite sweets."

He took the box, opened the lid, and found himself looking at Wiffer and Jeffer.

"Aaaugh!" he cried, and promptly dropped the box on the floor. Wiffer and Jeffer fell out on to the carpet, while the Reverend Cole did a sort of hobble-jump backwards, bumped straight into the coffee table, and knocked off the teapot that Mummy had just put there.

"Aaaugh!" cried the Reverend Cole again, as hot

tea splashed over his leg and foot. Then he hobble-hopped to an armchair, and hobble-slumped into it.

"Oh dear!" said Mummy. "I'm ever so sorry."

She fetched a couple of cloths, and while she wiped the Reverend Cole's shoe and trouser-leg, Daddy mopped up the tea from the carpet. Meanwhile, Wiffer and Jeffer lay next to the liquorice allsort box, and Jeremy James stood looking at them, with tears dropping out of his eyes.

Eventually, Daddy put them back in their box, Mummy made some more tea, and the Reverend Cole patted Jeremy James on the head.

"No harm done," he said. "Just a drop o' spilt tea. No need to cry."

Jeremy James hadn't been crying because of the spilt tea, but with Wiffer and Jeffer now safely back in their box, he stopped crying, and the Reverend Cole congratulated himself on his handling of the situation.

Daddy had dug a little grave under the apple tree, and very solemnly everyone trooped out into the garden. Mummy was holding Christopher, Daddy was holding Jennifer, Jeremy James was holding the box, and the Reverend Cole held forth:

"O Death," he said, "where is thy sting? O grave, where is thy victory? Oh Jeremy James, where is thy box?"

Jeremy James stepped forward with the box.

"Just put it in the . . . um . . . grave, will you?"

Jeremy James put the box in the grave.

"Forasmuch as the souls of these . . . um . . . gerbils here departed are in the care of Almighty God," said the Reverend Cole, "we therefore commit their bodies to the ground; earth to earth, ashes to ashes, dust to dust; in sure and certain . . . um . . . possible hope of eternal life, through our Lord Jesus Christ."

Beside the grave was a little pile of earth, which Daddy now pushed over the box until it was completely covered. Then the family went back into the house, and Mummy produced the sandwiches and cakes that were such an important part of any funeral.

"Will the gerbils be in Heaven now?" Jeremy James asked the Reverend Cole, through a mouthful of fruit cake.

"Ah!" said the Reverend Cole, through a mouthful

of salmon sandwich. "That's a very good question."

Since he showed no sign of answering it, Jeremy James asked him again.

"Many people do believe that animals have souls," he said, "and if they do, then I'm sure the gerbils will be in Heaven."

"What's a soul?" asked Jeremy James.

"It's the part of you that never dies," said the Reverend Cole. "It's your soul that goes to Heaven."

"Have I got one?" asked Jeremy James.

"Certainly," said the Reverend Cole.

"Where is it?" asked Jeremy James.

"Somewhere inside you," said the Reverend Cole. Jeremy James would have liked to ask a lot more questions about his soul, but Mummy and the Reverend Cole had to talk about the fête, and so Jeremy James turned his thoughts to fruit cake instead.

That night, Jeremy James couldn't get to sleep. He was thinking about the gerbils and Heaven and his soul. He had asked Mummy and Daddy where his soul was, but their answer had been just as vague as the Reverend Cole's: "Hmmph" (Mummy) and "Worple worple" (Daddy).

He'd also asked them where Heaven was. Mummy thought it might be somewhere beyond the stars, and Daddy thought it was the football ground after a home win.

The problem for Jeremy James was that if the

Reverend Cole was right, and the soul was inside you, it would have to get out and find its way to Heaven. How could it do that if it didn't know – or if you didn't know – where Heaven was? Daddy, for instance, couldn't even find his way round London, so how would *he* get to Heaven?

"I expect someone comes to guide you," Mummy had said.

And that was keeping Jeremy James awake. Nobody had come to guide the gerbils. They'd simply been lying in their cage, then they'd been put in the liquorice allsort box, and buried under the apple tree. He would have *seen* if anyone had come to guide them.

Great-Great-Aunt Maud had been buried on a Saturday. Jeremy James remembered that very well, because Daddy had wanted to go to a football match, and on their way home, they'd had to drive through the crowd. But she hadn't died on the Saturday. She'd died before. So why hadn't she been buried on the day she died?

The answer was obvious. You had to wait till the guide had come before you put the body in the box and buried it. But the gerbils *had* been buried on the day they'd died. And now their souls would be trying to get out of the box and out of the ground before the guide came, because otherwise he'd never find them, would go away, and they would never get to Heaven.

Jeremy James reached for his torch, climbed out

of bed, put on his slippers, and opened the bedroom door. The whole house was dark and silent. Everyone was asleep.

Jeremy James crept downstairs, unbolted the kitchen door, and made his way across the lawn to the apple tree.

The following morning, when she looked out of the kitchen window, Mummy was surprised to see a brightly coloured box lying under the apple tree. She knew at once what it was, and when she went out to take a closer look, she found the lid open, and the two gerbils inside, just as dead as ever. She hastily closed the lid, put the box back in its hole, and covered it up.

"I suppose it must have been a dog," she said to Daddy when he came downstairs.

"I shouldn't think a dog would have left them lying there," said Daddy.

But neither of them could think of a better explanation, and they agreed not to tell Jeremy James, because they didn't want to upset him.

Jeremy James didn't wake up till quite late that morning, but as soon as he went downstairs, he wanted to go and look at the gerbils' grave.

"A good thing you spotted it," said Daddy to Mummy, when Jeremy James had gone. "Imagine what he'd have felt if he'd seen them lying there."

When Jeremy James returned, there was a big smile on his face.

"You're looking very pleased with yourself," said Daddy.

And Jeremy James *was* pleased with himself. He knew that the guide had come in the night and taken the gerbils (and the liquorice allsort box) to Heaven. But he decided not to tell Mummy and Daddy. They didn't know enough about souls or about Heaven to really understand.

CHAPTER EIGHT

The Fête

The church fête was on Saturday. From Monday to Friday, the sun shone and the sky was a cloudless blue. Then on Saturday it rained.

"Would you believe it?" said Mummy.

"Yes," said Daddy.

"But the weather forecast was for sunshine," said Mummy.

"Then we should have known it would rain," said Daddy.

Mummy had spent all Friday evening baking cakes to sell to people who hadn't heard that cakes were bad for them.

"I don't know what we're going to do with all these cakes if we don't sell them," she said.

Jeremy James knew what *he* would do with them, given half a chance. And he was sure Daddy and the twins would help him. He even offered to start straight away, but Mummy said, "We'll wait and see", which meant no.

Daddy carried the cakes through the wind and rain, and loaded them into the car ("They've all

turned into Bath buns," he said), while Jeremy James and the twins were wrapped up in their hooded anoraks. Then with Mummy carrying Christopher, Daddy carrying Jennifer, and Jeremy James carrying himself, they all made a splashing dash to the car.

"Jeffer wet!" announced Jennifer.

"Wiffer wet!" announced Christopher.

"Everybody wet," said Daddy. "They should have invited Noah to be guest of honour."

The guest of honour was in fact to be the Right Honourable Cecil Ponsonby-Thistlethwaite, MP, who – as Daddy explained to Jeremy James – was a politician.

Jeremy James had seen some politicians before, when Daddy had taken him to London.

"Is he one of those that's ruining the country?" he asked.

"He is indeed," said Daddy. "And if he makes a speech, he'll probably ruin the fête as well. If the rain hasn't ruined it already."

The rain was coming down harder than ever, and the wind was huffing and puffing like a pack of little-piggy wolves. The field was a thick and squelchy rug of mud, but someone had built a wooden pathway from the car-park to the big marquee, where the fête would now take place. Daddy carried the cakes, Mummy wheeled the twins in their push-chair, and Jeremy James hung on to Mummy's coat, as the wind blew them all the way to the marquee.

"Ah, there you are!" said the Reverend Cole. "What a day! The Lord must have got his dates mixed up!"

"Maybe He's telling us to cancel," said Daddy.

"No, no, we can't cancel," said the Reverend Cole. "The MP will be here soon."

"Maybe that's why the Lord wants us to cancel," said Daddy.

All round the marquee, people were setting up their stalls, and at one end there was a little platform on which a man in overalls was standing at a microphone. It kept making whistling and crackling noises, and the man kept saying, "Testing! Testing! Can you hear me?"

Daddy and Jeremy James both shouted yes.

"Thank you," said the man.

85

"Why does he want us to hear him?" asked Jeremy James.

"Because there's going to be a speech," said Daddy.

"Still testing," said the man. "Testing, testing."

"That's a boring speech," said Jeremy James.

Meanwhile, more people came trickling and dripping into the marquee, while the rain pounded against the roof, and the wind made the sides flap in and out as if they were taking deep breaths.

Suddenly there was a flurry of activity, as the Reverend Cole hurried like a lame tortoise towards a couple who had just come in. He arrived in time to take the man's hat and coat, and the lady's coat and umbrella.

The man was fat and bald, and wore a grey suit with a blue flower in the buttonhole. The lady was tall and thin, and wore a blue dress with white spots, and a white hat with blue spots. They made their way across the marquee, and as they came level with Jeremy James, the tall thin lady gave him a tall thin smile, and touched her husband's arm.

"Ah! A little boy," said the fat man. "Hello, little boy. How are you today?"

He really was very fat. His stomach was pressing hard against the closed buttons of his jacket, and Jeremy James wondered how far the buttons would go if they burst.

"Very well, thank you," said Jeremy James.

86

"Good," said the fat man. "You know who I am, don't you?"

"You're a Polly Tishun," said Jeremy James.

"That's right!" cried the fat man. "Well done! And you know what politicians do?"

"Yes," said Jeremy James. "They ruin the country."

"What?" said the fat man.

"They ruin the country," said Jeremy James again.

"Nonsense!" said the fat man. "Who's been telling you such nonsense?"

"Daddy," said Jeremy James.

Daddy turned a little red and shuffled his feet.

"Let me tell you," said the fat man, "this government is doing a splendid job, and everything in the garden is coming up roses."

"You mustn't tell fibs," said Jeremy James.

"I'm not telling fibs," said the fat man.

"Yes you are," said Jeremy James.

"No I'm not," said the fat man.

"Come along, dear," said the tall thin lady. "This is no time for a political discussion."

"There's always time for a political discussion," said the fat man. "Besides, the children of today are the voters of tomorrow."

"Well, you can worry about that tomorrow," said the tall thin lady.

The fat man frowned and looked straight at Daddy.

"You shouldn't tell your little boy such things," he said.

"Well if everything in the garden *was* coming up roses," said Daddy, "I wouldn't have to."

The fat man said something rather like "Hmmph!", and jelly-wobbled away.

"He does tell fibs, doesn't he Daddy?" asked Jeremy James.

"He certainly does," said Daddy.

"*And* he eats too many wrong things," said Jeremy James.

The Reverend Cole's legs heaved his body up the steps on to the platform, and the MP and his wife followed.

"Ah! Foof! Foof!" cried the Reverend Cole into the microphone. "Can you . . . ah . . . can you hear me?"

There were a few nods and cries of yes, including a loud one from Jeremy James.

"Let us begin with a short prayer," continued the Reverend Cole. "O almighty and most merciful God, of thy bountiful goodness keep us, we beseech thee, from all things that may hurt us . . ."

"Especially rain and politicians," murmured Daddy.

" . . . that we, being ready both in body and soul, may cheerfully accomplish those things that Thou wouldst have done; through Jesus Christ our Lord."

There was a murmur of "Amen".

"What *is* 'Ah men'?" asked Jeremy James.

"The opposite of 'Ah women'," said Daddy.

"It means something like 'Let it be true'," said Mummy.

The Reverend Cole then welcomed everybody, and introduced the Right Honourable Cecil Ponsonby-Thistlethwaite MP, "just to say a few words".

"Amen," said Daddy.

"Lovely to see you all," said the fat man, "in spite of this dreadful weather. Please don't blame the government for that, ha ha!"

He waited for people to laugh, but nobody did. Then he went on to talk about himself and about the government, and about the government and about himself, and about how wonderful the government was, and about how wonderful he was, and . . . Jeremy James stopped listening and looked round the marquee.

There were quite a lot of people now, and they all seemed rather miserable. It was difficult to say if they were miserable because they were wet, or miserable because they were bored.

"I and the government will go on doing what's right and what's good . . ." said the fat man.

"This," murmured Daddy, "is a fête worse than death."

The wind screamed, and the rain drummed, but not even they could drown the endless drone of the fat man.

It was at this moment that Jeremy James happened to look up, and having looked up, he stayed looking up. What he saw reminded him very strongly of the fortune-teller. High above the head of the fat man, the roof of the marquee seemed to be bulging downwards, and there was a gap appearing between the roof and the side, as if an invisible hand was slowly pulling the two sections apart.

Jeremy James tugged Daddy's sleeve. Daddy looked down.

"Boring, eh?" whispered Daddy.

Jeremy James shook his head and pointed upwards. Daddy followed the direction of the point, and his eyes widened.

"Good Lord!" he said.

Jeremy James had not seen Daddy move so fast since Timothy had got stuck in the sea and Daddy had had to rush out and rescue him.

"Get off!" Daddy shouted, as he neared the platform. "Get off!"

". . . because the fact is, we know what's best for everyone . . ." the fat man was saying.

Daddy jumped up on to the platform, pointed upwards, and at once the Reverend Cole and the tall thin lady hurried down the steps.

"Cecil!" cried the lady.

". . . and you can put your trust in us—"

"Cecil!"

"Ssh! I'm talking, dear! And get that wretched man away from me! Damned Opposition agitators

everywhere. Believe me, ladies and gentlemen, we know what we're doing, and your future is utterly safe in our—"

But nobody heard what their future was utterly safe in, because at that precise moment, the bulge in the roof turned into an open flap, and down came a great swooshing cataract of water. It had one target only: the Right Honourable Cecil Ponsonby-Thistlethwaite.

The drenching took only a couple of seconds, but at the end of it, the fat man was standing on the platform soaked through from head to toe, and dripping like a giant sponge.

At once some kind souls hurried to help him, and he was led away gasping and spluttering.

"Thank you so much for saving me," the tall thin lady said to Daddy.

"It wasn't me," said Daddy. "It was Jeremy James who spotted it."

The lady came across to Jeremy James.

"I understand it was you who spotted the danger," she said.

"Yes," said Jeremy James.

"You're a very smart young man," said the lady, "and I want to thank you."

With that she reached into her purse, and pulled out a five pound note.

Jeremy James's eyes went as wide as the flap in the roof, and he gasped almost as loud as the fat man had done.

"Five pounds!" he cried. "Thank you very much!"

"When you grow up," said the lady, with the thinnest of thin smiles, "I think I might well be voting for you."

Then she hurried away to be with her husband.

Next it was the Reverend Cole who wanted to say thank you.

"Actually," he said to Daddy, "when you were shouting 'Get off!' I thought you were trying to stop him talking."

"It was a temptation," said Daddy. "But as things turned out, he stopped talking anyway, didn't he?"

"Ah!" said the Reverend Cole. "God moves in a mysterious way his wonders to perform."

Then the Reverend Cole thanked Jeremy James for spotting the danger, and put his hand in his pocket. Jeremy James began to go wide-eyed again, but instead of a five pound note, out came a handkerchief.

"Well done, Jeremy James," he said, wiping his nose. "You'll get your reward in Heaven."

The church fête really was ruined by the weather, and after the accident with the roof, most people wanted to leave the marquee as quickly as possible anyway. The guest of honour had wanted to leave it even more quickly than possible, and was not seen again that afternoon. But although the occasion had been such a disaster, everyone agreed that it had also been quite memorable. Certainly Mummy and Daddy were not the only people who were still laughing when they got home.

As for Jeremy James, he thought the fête had been a great success, and to prove it he had a five pound note and as many cakes as he could eat.

Never Steal
wheels from
a Dog

For Ruth Weibel,
with love and thanks

Contents

CHAPTER ONE

The Patch

'Oh no!' cried Daddy. 'Look at this! What a disaster!'

Mummy and Jeremy James both came running to the bathroom, where Daddy stood pale-faced in front of the mirror.

'What's happened?' asked Mummy.

'Look!' said Daddy. 'Just look!'

He held out his comb. Mummy looked, and then Jeremy James looked.

'It's just a comb with a few hairs in it,' said Mummy.

'A few?' cried Daddy. 'There's a whole handful!'

He pulled them out of the comb, and laid them in his hand.

'Your hand isn't full,' said Jeremy James.

'That's not the point,' said Daddy. 'It's the space left on my head that I'm worried about.'

He ran his comb through his hair again, had a look, and let out more groans.

'Let's see your head,' said Mummy.

Daddy bent over.

'Yes, there is a thin bit here,' said Mummy.

'Oh no! How thin is it?' wailed Daddy.

'Just a bit thin,' said Mummy. 'Thinning rather than thin.'

'Can I see?' asked Jeremy James.

Daddy bent his head a little lower.

'I can see your skin,' said Jeremy James.

'I knew it!' said Daddy. 'Once it starts, there's no stopping it.'

'What is it?' asked Jeremy James.

'Baldness,' said Daddy. 'That's what it is. I'm losing my hair.'

'Shall I help you find it?' asked Jeremy James.

'When it's gone, it's gone,' moaned Daddy. 'A little bald patch becomes a bigger bald patch, and before you know it, the jungle's turned into a desert.'

He went into the bedroom, where there was a

mirror with three movable parts that enabled you to look at the back of your own head. Meanwhile, Mummy and Jeremy James went to the twins' room.

'Mama! Jem-Jem!' cried Jennifer, standing in her cot.

'Mama! Jem-Jem!' said Christopher, lying in his cot.

Babies were lucky. All they knew about was being washed, dressed and fed. They had no idea of the disaster that had struck the family. But Jeremy James had seen bald people before, and once he'd been to the hairdresser's and had nearly been balded himself. It had been a pretty frightening experience.

'Is Daddy really going to be balded?' he asked Mummy.

'I expect so, eventually,' said Mummy, lifting Jennifer out of her cot. 'Baldness happens to a lot of men. Daddy's father was also bald.'

Now that was *really* frightening. Daddy's father was dead.

'Did Daddy's father die because he was balded?' asked Jeremy James.

'No, of course not,' said Mummy, lifting Christopher out of his cot. 'Baldness never killed anybody.'

There were more groans from the bedroom. Baldness might never kill anybody, but it was certainly hurting Daddy.

'Am I going to be balded too?' asked Jeremy James.

'Perhaps,' said Mummy, 'but don't start worrying about it now.'

Jeremy James *was* worried. He liked having his hair. He felt that his hair was a part of him. If he didn't have his hair, he would be ... well ... balded. And he didn't want to be balded.

Back in his room, he looked at himself in the mirror and put his hands on top of his head to cover the hair. Then he took his hands away again. No doubt about it, he looked a lot better with his hair than without it. But Daddy was going bald, and Daddy's father had gone bald (and died). And when Jeremy James ran his comb over his head and found not one but *two* hairs in it, his hopes of a hairy future looked thin rather than thinning.

In the course of the day, Jeremy James asked both Mummy and Daddy what could be done to stop hair from falling out. The gist of their replies was 'No idea' (Daddy) and 'That's enough about hair' (Mummy).

'But what are *you* going to do, Daddy?' persisted Jeremy James.

'There's nothing anyone *can* do,' said Daddy sadly. 'That's life, Jeremy James. Hair today, and gone tomorrow.'

Daddy always said there was nothing you could do, but that was because Daddy wasn't very good at doing things. He wasn't very good at mending cars, or knocking in nails, or changing dirty nappies. And so of course he wouldn't be very good at saving hair – Jeremy James's or his own. Jeremy James would have to get help from someone else.

Mr Drew, the kind man who ran the sweet shop,

had a lot of hair which was grey, but when Jeremy James paid him a chocolate-buying visit and popped the vital question, Mr Drew said he never did anything to stop his hair from falling out. It just stayed on of its own accord.

'Will mine stay on its own cord as well?' asked Jeremy James.

'I don't know,' said Mr Drew. 'It's like your ears,' he said. 'You can't change your ears, can you?'

'No,' said Jeremy James.

'Well, you can't change your hair either,' said Mr Drew.

The situation seemed to be getting worse.

'Are my ears going to fall off as well, then?' asked Jeremy James.

Mr Drew assured him that his ears would stay where they were. It was only hair that fell out, and some people had falling-out hair and some people had staying-on hair, and there was nothing you could do to change it.

'But what you *can* do,' said Mr Drew, 'is suck this lollipop.'

'Will that help my hair to stay on?' asked Jeremy James.

'No,' said Mr Drew, 'but it'll take your mind off it.'

Jeremy James's mind went on and off the subject of falling hair for two or three days – in fact, until Jennifer had an accident with her doll.

'Jeffer dolly boken!' she cried one afternoon.

'Jeffer dolly leg boken!' said Christopher, with a keen eye for detail.

Sure enough, one of dolly's legs lay bodiless on the floor of the playpen. Her condition looked serious, and Daddy was summoned from his study to deal with the emergency. To Jeremy James's surprise, he did not say that there was nothing he could do. He took the doll from Jennifer, picked up the lonely leg, examined it, and informed the crowd of on-lookers (Mummy, Jeremy James, Jennifer and Christopher) that he would perform the leg-saving operation immediately.

He went into the kitchen, and returned with a little tube in his hand. He opened the tube, and squeezed a bit of something onto the top of dolly's leg. Then he squeezed some more something round the hole where dolly's leg should have been.

'Now we wait,' he said, with the calm authority of a master surgeon at work.

Everyone waited. Nothing happened. Daddy simply stood there with the doll in one hand and the leg in the other.

'Give dolly leg!' cried Jennifer, losing patience.

'Right, everybody,' said Daddy. 'I want you all to close your eyes, and keep them closed until I tell you to open them.'

Everybody (except Mummy) closed their eyes.

'Now say out loud: "Make dolly's leg better!" '

Everybody (including Mummy) said: 'Make dolly's leg better!'

'Keep your eyes closed,' said Daddy, 'just a few more seconds . . . and . . . open your eyes.'

Jeremy James, Jennifer and Christopher opened

their eyes. Dolly's leg was back on. And what was even more magical, it stayed on, even when Jennifer pulled it.

'What's in the tube, Daddy?' asked Jeremy James.

'A glue called Stick-It,' said Daddy. 'And as you can see, Stick-It stuck it.'

It was at this moment that Jeremy James had a bright idea. When Daddy returned to the kitchen, he followed him, and watched him put the Stick-It tube in the middle drawer of the cupboard.

'Can Stick-It stick anything?' he asked.

'Anything and everything,' said Daddy.

Jeremy James's idea seemed even brighter.

He waited until Daddy had gone back to his study, and Mummy was reading in the armchair, then he slipped into the kitchen, took the tube of glue from the drawer, and went up to his room.

There he carefully undid the top, bent his head, pushed the tube through his hair till he could feel it on his scalp, and squeezed. Then he moved the tube backwards and sideways and forwards and round and all over until he'd covered his whole head. Some of the glue got onto his fingers too.

Jeremy James looked at himself in the mirror. There was nothing to see, except a sort of shininess on his hair. What next? He had to wait. And so he sat on the bed and waited long enough to want to stop waiting. Then he closed his eyes, and said: 'Make Jeremy James's hair stick.'

When he looked at himself in the mirror again, he saw that his hair was now in sticky clumps with blobs of white on them, and he was also beginning to get a funny feeling on the top of his head – rather hot and tight, as if someone was scrunching it. He put his hand on his head to give it a rub, but his hand got stuck. He pulled, but it wouldn't come away. Maybe the bright idea hadn't been so bright after all.

When Jeremy James went downstairs into the living room, Mummy looked up from her book and screamed as if she'd just seen a giant mouse.

'What's happened to your hair?' she shrieked.

'I put Stick-It on it,' said Jeremy James.

'Oh good heavens!' cried Mummy. 'Take your hand away and let me see.'

'I can't,' said Jeremy James. 'It's stuck.'

Mummy screamed again, and Daddy rushed in from his study.

'What is it? What's wrong? What's happened? Good Lord!' cried Daddy.

Mummy told him about the Stick-It.

'What are we going to do?' she asked.

'There's nothing we can do,' said Daddy. 'He'll have to see a doctor.'

Within two minutes Jeremy James was strapped in the back of the car, his hand still firmly stuck to the top of his head, and he and Daddy were on their way to the hospital.

'What an unusual hairstyle!' said the grey-haired lady at the desk, when Daddy and Jeremy James arrived. 'Haven't I seen you before?'

She had. Jeremy James had been to the hospital not long ago, with a sprained wrist, and he'd got lost

looking for a fish tank. Half the staff had been searching for him, and in the end they'd had to call the police.

'Yes, I pained my wrist,' said Jeremy James.

'As I remember,' said the grey-haired lady, 'that wasn't the only thing you pained. And what have you been up to this time?'

Daddy explained the sticky situation to her, and then he and Jeremy James sat down to wait for the doctor.

After a few minutes a rosy-cheeked nurse in a blue uniform came walking across the room.

'Oh, it's the lost boy!' she cried. 'And now what have you done to yourself?'

Jeremy James told the nurse what had happened, and she took him and Daddy to see the doctor.

'Oh, it's the fish tank boy!' cried the doctor. 'Another hair-raising adventure, I see. What's the story this time?'

Jeremy James told the doctor what had happened, and he looked at his hand, looked at his head, and gave some instructions to the nurse, who left.

The doctor was wearing a white coat, and he had blue eyes and red hair which was thin rather than thinning.

'To stop your hair falling out, eh?' he said. 'Well, let me know if it works.'

He left too, and the rosy-cheeked nurse returned with a towel, a sponge, a little bottle, a razor, a pair of scissors, and a teaspoon. She filled the sink with hot water, and poured the contents of the bottle into it. The water became very bubbly. Then she put the towel round Jeremy James's shoulders and asked Daddy to lift him up so that his head and hand were bent over the sink.

'Dip your head, Jeremy James,' she said.

The hot bubbly water felt nice and soothing as the nurse sponged it over him, and very gently she began to ease his fingers off his head with the handle of the teaspoon.

'Right,' she said, when the last finger had been spooned free. 'That was the nice bit. Now comes the nasty bit.'

She dried his hair, sat him in a chair, and picked up the scissors.

'Oh dear!' said Daddy.

'Oh no!' said Jeremy James.

'Afraid so!' said the nurse.

With loud snips of her scissors, she cut off great chunks of tangled hair, which fell silently to the floor at Jeremy James's feet.

'We're going to shave the rest,' she told Daddy, 'so that we can get the glue off his scalp.'

By the time she'd finished snipping, shaving, washing and sponging Jeremy James's head, it wasn't sticky any more, and the tight feeling had gone.

'Do you want to see it?' asked the nurse.

She fetched a mirror, and what Jeremy James saw was his own face underneath a very smooth, very shiny egg. And the eyes below the egg began to send out a few shiny tears. He'd been balded.

'Some barbers would charge you twenty pounds for that,' said Daddy.

'It's quite fashionable,' said the nurse. 'My cousin's best friend's sister's boyfriend's brother has it cut that way. And, in any case, it'll soon grow again, Jeremy James.'

After a few weeks, Jeremy James's hair had indeed grown again, and it looked just like before. In the meantime, though, Daddy had lost some more handfuls, and the thin patch had become a little thinner and a little wider. *His* hair wasn't growing again.

Jeremy James asked why his own hair had grown and Daddy's had not, but Daddy just mumbled that it was all a matter of 'worple, worple genetics', which meant that he didn't know. Jeremy James, however, had a pretty good idea of the reason. He'd put Stick-It on his head, and Daddy hadn't.

CHAPTER TWO

The Thingummy

It was a remarkable thingummy. No one had ever seen one like it. Without a doubt, it was the best thingummy ever made, and it belonged to Timothy Smyth-Fortescue, who was the cleverest, handsomest, strongest and wonderfullest boy Timothy Smyth-Fortescue had ever known.

He lived in the house next door to Jeremy James's, but his house was much bigger than Jeremy James's and, according to Timothy, it was also much nicer, warmer, posher and grander. His house was more like a palace than a house, and any king and queen would be proud to live there. In fact, a king did live there: his name was Timothy Smyth-Fortescue.

The thingummy was small and red with a white cross on it, and although it looked like a pocket-knife, it wasn't a pocket-knife because it was full of whatsits. Timothy's father had brought it back from a place called Sweaterland, where there were a lot of mountains and snow, and people needed special thingummies in case they got caught in an afterlunch.

'What's an afterlunch?' asked Jeremy James.

'You don't know anything, do you?' sneered Timothy. 'An afterlunch is when a lot of snow falls in the afternoon, and people can't go out.'

'Why can't they go out?' asked Jeremy James.

'Because if it snows in the afternoon, you can catch your life of cold.'

'My mummy says you catch your *death* of cold,' said Jeremy James.

'How can you catch your death of cold?' scoffed Timothy. 'You'd be dead if you caught your death of cold. Your mummy isn't dead, is she?'

Jeremy James had to agree that she wasn't.

They were sitting in Timothy's room, which was a wonderful room full of wonderful things, as was right and proper for such a wonderful boy, and Timothy now showed Jeremy James all the wonderful pieces of his wonderful thingummy. It had a tin-opener, a bottle-opener, a nail file, scissors, a saw, a needle, a torch . . .

'Does the torch work?' asked Jeremy James.

'Of course it works,' said Timothy, and shone it straight into Jeremy James's eyes.

Jeremy James had to admit that it really was wonderful, and he wished *he* had one, and could he hold it?

'No,' said Timothy. 'You're too young to hold it. It's only for grown-ups. Like me.'

'You're not a grown-up!' said Jeremy James.

'Yes I am,' said Timothy, 'cos I'm older and bigger than you *and* I've got freckles.'

Jeremy James didn't see why having freckles

should make anyone . . . However, at that moment there was a knock on the door.

'Who is it?' called Timothy.

'It's Mummy, darling. Can I come in?'

'Yes, all right,' said Timothy, and in came Mrs Smyth-Fortescue.

'Hello, darlings,' she said. 'I'm just going down to the shops, so I'm sure you'll be all right on your own, won't you? I'll only be a minute, and Daddy's somewhere around, if he hasn't popped off to America.'

'Get me some chocolate, then,' said Timothy.

'Only if you say please, dear,' said Mrs Smyth-Fortescue.

'Get me some chocolate, pzzz,' said Timothy.

'There's a good boy. And look after little Jeremy. You'll be all right, Jeremy, won't you?' (Mrs Smyth-Fortescue never called him Jeremy *James*.)

'Yes, thank you, Mrs Smyth-Fatticoo.' (Jeremy James never called her Mrs Smyth-*Fortescue*.)

'Be good then, darlings, and I'll be back very soon.'

With a smile and a wave she was gone.

'Can't I just hold it for a minute?' asked Jeremy James.

'No,' said Timothy, 'but I'll show you how it works if you like.'

Jeremy James did like. At least, he thought he liked.

'Hold out your hand,' said Timothy.

Jeremy James wasn't quite so sure that he liked. There were some very sharp bits on the thingummy.

113

'Hold out your hand!' repeated Timothy.

'What are you going to do?' asked Jeremy James.

'Hold out your hand and you'll see,' said Timothy.

Jeremy James held out his hand, and then he pulled it back again.

'I don't want my hand cutted off!' he said.

'Your hand isn't going to be cutted off, stupid,' said Timothy. 'I'm going to file your nail.'

'Well I don't want my nail fileded either,' said Jeremy James.

He didn't know what nail-filing was, but he was taking no chances. Timothy called him stupid again, and then held the file against his own nail and rasped it up and down.

'See!' he sneered.

He held out his finger and Jeremy James saw that the finger-nail was sort of crooked, with a bit missing down the side.

'It looks funny,' he said.

'No it doesn't,' said Timothy. 'That's what grown-ups do. You kids don't know how to file your nails.'

'My mummy and daddy *cut* their nails,' said Jeremy James.

'Well I can cut nails too!' said Timothy, and snipped the air with the scissors part of the thingum-my. Then he snipped a scrap of paper that was lying on the carpet, and he snipped the sheet hanging down from his bed, and he snipped a leg of Jeremy James's trousers.

'Ow!' cried Jeremy James. 'You cutted my trousers!'

114

'Cutted trousers don't hurt!' scoffed Timothy. 'Look!'

He cut a hole in his own trousers.

'See!' he said. 'It doesn't hurt at all. Bet you don't know what this is.'

Jeremy James didn't know.

'It's a scoodiver.'

'What does it do?'

'It dives scoos. Watch.'

Timothy stood up, and went to a shelf on the wall. There were some books and ornaments on the shelf, but Timothy ignored those. Instead, he started turning something underneath the shelf. After a lot of turning, and grunting and oofing, he finally pulled something out of the wall.

'There!' he said, and held out his hand with a screw in it. As he did so, there was a loud creak, the shelf suddenly swung downwards, and all the books and ornaments fell with a crash to the floor.

'What a scoodiver!' cried Timothy.

'What a mess!' cried Jeremy James.

'Oh, my mum'll clear that up,' said Timothy. 'You know what this is?'

Jeremy James did know this time, because he'd seen Daddy use something like it once.

'It's a saw,' he said.

'Let's find some wood,' said Timothy. 'Come on. I know where I can find some.'

He led the way downstairs into the living room, in one corner of which stood a large piano.

'You're not going to seesaw the piano, are you?' gasped Jeremy James.

'I could if I wanted to,' said Timothy. 'But I'll do this instead.'

He knelt down next to the piano stool, and sawed away at one leg. His face went quite red, but after a few buzzy scrapes amid a little cloud of woody powder, the stool suddenly did a knees-bend and toppled over right beside him and beside its sawn-off leg.

'You're going to get into trouble,' said Jeremy James.

'No I'm not,' said Timothy, 'cos that's what a thingummy is for. My dad wouldn't have given it to me if I wasn't supposed to use it, would he?'

That was true, but Jeremy James didn't think Timothy should be using it on the furniture.

'It's only an old piano stool,' said Timothy. 'My mum said it's over a hundred years old, so they should get a new one, shouldn't they?'

Timothy next led the way to the kitchen, where he used the tin-opener to open a tin, the bottle-opener to open a bottle, and then . . .

'What is it?' asked Jeremy James.

'It's a corkscoo,' said Timothy. 'You scoo corks with it. And I know where the corks are.'

He opened a door, and Jeremy James saw a flight of steps leading down into the darkness.

'Let's go down into the cellar,' said Timothy. 'That's where my dad keeps his wine.'

But Jeremy James didn't much fancy the idea of going down into the darkness with Timothy. He'd been trapped in a cellar once before, in Mrs Gullick's house at Warkin-on-Sea, and that had been frightening enough even without Timothy. Besides, he didn't really want to be there when Mrs Smyth-Fortescue came home and found the broken shelf and the cut sheet and trousers, and the three-legged piano stool, and the open tin and bottle . . .

'I've got to go home,' he said, and ran out of the kitchen, into the hall, and into a stomach which sent an OOF up to the mouth high above it. The stomach, mouth and OOF belonged to a man with red hair and freckles.

'Where are you rushing to, my boy?' asked Mr Smyth-Fortescue.

'I've got to go home,' said Jeremy James, 'and

I never touched the shelf and the stool and the bottle . . . '

'Shelf, stool, bottle?' asked Mr Smyth-Fortescue.

' . . . and Timothy's trousers . . . '

'Where *is* Timothy?' asked Mr Smyth-Fortescue.

'In the cellar,' said Jeremy James, 'and I've got to go home.'

'What's he doing in the cellar?' asked Mr Smyth-Fortescue.

'Scooing corks,' said Jeremy James, 'and please can I go home?'

Mr Smyth-Fortescue opened the front door, and Jeremy James went home.

He didn't see Timothy for some time after that, but one day, when he and Mummy were out shopping, they bumped into Mrs Smyth-Fortescue and Timothy. While the two mothers had a quick conversation about the weather, the price of clothes, Mrs G. from over the road, Mr R. just round the corner, Timothy's school report, the bus service, Mrs L.'s daughter who should have known better, a recipe for disaster, and how time flies, Jeremy James asked Timothy if he had his thingummy with him.

'No,' said Timothy.

'Where is it then?' asked Jeremy James.

Timothy's bottom lip took a step forward, and his eyes threw a sort of saw-and-scissors look at Mrs Smyth-Fortescue.

'They took it away,' he said.

Just for a moment, Jeremy James thought

of asking Mrs Smyth-Fortescue if he could have it, but he didn't.

'I know why they took it away,' he said.

'No you don't,' said Timothy.

'Yes I do,' said Jeremy James. 'It's cos you're too young to have a thingummy.'

'No I'm not,' said Timothy. 'It's cos when they saw what I could do with it, they wanted it for themselves.'

Jeremy James had also wanted it for himself, so he might have believed Timothy. But he didn't.

CHAPTER THREE

Get the Erker

Round-faced Richard was Jeremy James's best friend, and sometimes he came to Jeremy James's house, but most times Jeremy James had to go to his house because of Gran.

Gran was very old, and since Richard's mother and father both went out to work, she was supposed to look after Richard during the day. Richard said it was the other way round: he had to look after Gran. She was always wanting things, and that meant he was always fetching things.

'It's because of me legs,' she kept saying. 'I can't move because of me legs.'

Jeremy James thought that most people *could* move because of their legs, but Gran's legs were special. To use them she needed a stick, and once Jeremy James and Richard had helped her and her stick to go to the lavatory, where she'd got locked in. Jeremy James had tried to rescue her, but in the end Mr Biddles from next door had had to rescue Gran *and* Jeremy James.

'Hello, dearie,' said Gran, when Jeremy James arrived to play with Richard. 'You was the lad what got locked in the lavat'ry, wasn't you?'

Maybe Gran needed a stick for her memory as well.

'*You* got locked in the lavatory, Gran!' said Jeremy James. 'And I helped to rescue you.'

"'Ope yer've already been this time.'

Gran's hearing was about as good as her walking and her memory.

'Just pass me the zapper, Richard dear, will yer, an' switch the telly on for me.'

Since it was raining outside, Richard and Jeremy James went upstairs to play.

'Richard, dear!' came Gran's voice just as they'd reached the landing. 'I can't find me cigarettes!'

Richard and Jeremy James went downstairs again, and found Gran's cigarettes in the kitchen.

'Maybe we shouldn't give them to her,' whispered Richard. 'My mum says smoking's bad for her.'

"'Ave yer found 'em, dear?'

'She'll only make us keep looking,' said Jeremy James.

'Yes,' said Richard. 'And if we couldn't find them, she'd send us out to buy some.'

Back to the living room they went, and Richard handed over the packet.

'There's a good boy,' said Gran. 'An' don't tell yer mother. Off yer go now an' play wiv yer friend. Only keep 'im out o' the lavat'ry. Give us the matches before yer go, an' the ashtray.'

Richard fetched the matches, while Jeremy James fetched the ashtray.

121

'I'd get 'em meself, dear,' said Gran, 'only I can't becos of me legs.'

Once more Richard and Jeremy James went upstairs, and Richard left the door open just in case Gran called.

'She's nice really,' said Richard. 'She just doesn't *seem* very nice.'

Richard had a lot of games and toys and, unlike Timothy, he liked sharing them. He also had a bar of chocolate, and he shared that as well. A friend who shares a bar of chocolate is a friend indeed. The afternoon was passing very pleasantly, and they were just finishing the last couple of squares when Richard noticed something.

'What is it?' asked Jeremy James.

'Listen,' said Richard.

Jeremy James listened. All he could hear was the noise from the TV downstairs.

'That's all I can hear too,' said Richard.

There didn't seem to be much of a mystery.

'Well,' said Richard, 'Gran hasn't asked me to do anything. And she always asks me to do things.'

'Maybe she's asleep,' said Jeremy James.

But when they crept downstairs and peeped into the living room, Gran was not asleep. They knew she wasn't asleep because her eyes were wide open. On the other hand, she wasn't watching the television either, because she was lying back in her chair looking at the ceiling.

'Are you all right, Gran?' called Richard from the doorway.

Gran didn't say that she wasn't all right, but nor did she say that she was. She just went on staring up at the ceiling.

'She looks a bit funny,' said Richard.

'She looks a bit dead,' said Jeremy James.

Jeremy James had seen dead things before: his two gerbils had died, and although Gran didn't look like a gerbil, she was all stiff like them, and they'd had their eyes open too.

Richard started to cry, and then Jeremy James started to cry as well. A dead Gran would really ruin the afternoon for both of them. For Gran as well. And there were things you were supposed to do when people died.

'Maybe we should put her in a box,' said Jeremy James.

Great-Aunt Maud had been put in a box, and Jeremy James himself had buried the gerbils in a liquorice all-sorts packet.

'Have you got a big box?' he asked Richard.

'What for?' asked Richard through his tears.

'Cos you have to put dead people in boxes,' said Jeremy James.

'My train set came in a big box,' said Richard, 'but I don't think it's big enough for Gran.'

'I think it has to be a wooden box anyway,' said Jeremy James, 'cos my great-aunt Maud was in a wooden box.'

'We could put her in my tree-house,' suggested Richard. 'That's a sort of wooden box.'

'I don't think I could carry Gran up a tree,' said Jeremy James. 'And anyway it's raining. She'd catch her life of cold.'

'So what are we going to do?' wailed Richard.

'Well,' said Jeremy James, remembering something else about his dead gerbils, 'maybe we shouldn't do anything till someone comes to take her soul to Heaven.'

Not doing anything seemed a good idea. The more nothing you do, the less difficult it is to do it, and they would both have happily gone on doing nothing if something hadn't suddenly moved in Gran's right hand. It was a cigarette falling. And it fell onto the carpet beside Gran's chair. The two boys watched with fascination from the doorway as smoke began to rise. Then with a little puff, the smoke turned into a flame.

Jeremy James had never seen Richard waddle so fast. He crossed the room, picked up a rug, and threw it over the flame. Then he beat at it with both hands.

'She's done this before,' he said, as Jeremy James joined him. 'One day she'll be burneded alive.'

'Or burneded dead,' said Jeremy James.

It was at this moment that Jeremy James noticed something strange about Gran. Although her head and body didn't move, her eyes did. It was as if she was trying to look at Richard beating out the fire. And then from one corner of her almost-closed mouth came a hoarse whisper: 'Get the . . . ' But the next word was impossible to hear.

'She's alive!' said Jeremy James.

Richard stopped hitting the rug, and they both looked at Gran. There was no doubt about it. Her eyes were moving, and again she groaned: 'Get the . . . ' whatever it was.

'She probably wants another cigarette,' said Richard.

Gran made a moaning noise.

'I don't think you should give it to her,' said Jeremy James.

'Get the erer,' moaned Gran.

'What's an erer?' asked Richard.

'I don't know,' said Jeremy James.

Gran closed her eyes.

'She's going to sleep,' said Richard.

Gran opened her eyes.

'No she's not,' said Jeremy James.

Gran seemed to take a deep breath, looked

125

straight at Richard (though still not moving her head), and with a great effort groaned: 'Get the erker!'

'I can't, Gran,' said Richard, close to tears again. 'I don't know what an erker is!'

Jeremy James wondered if he should run home and ask Mummy and Daddy what an erer or erker was, but then his mind went back to a hotel room in London, where he and Daddy had once stayed. Daddy had gone out to the lavatory, and Jeremy James had pressed the 9 button on the telephone three times and spoken to a nice lady. She had sent a policeman, a policewoman and an ambulance round to keep him company. Maybe she would help him again.

Richard thought that was a good idea, and so Jeremy James went to the telephone in the corner of the room and pressed the 9 button three times. Immediately a woman's voice asked: 'Police, fire or ambulance?'

Jeremy James didn't think he needed the police, because Gran hadn't actually done anything naughty. Fire might be more useful, except that the fire was out now.

'Ampulus!' he decided.

There were a few clicks, and then another woman asked him his name. Jeremy James was a bit surprised that she didn't remember him. She also wanted his telephone number and address, and Jeremy James explained that he wasn't at home now, he was at Richard's.

'Is Richard ill?' asked the woman.

'No,' said Jeremy James, 'I don't think so. Are you ill, Richard?'

'No,' said Richard.

'No,' Jeremy James told the lady. 'But Gran wants an erer or an erker, and we don't know what it is.'

'Is Gran there?' asked the lady.

'Yes,' said Jeremy James.

'Can I speak to her, then?' asked the lady.

'Gran can't move,' said Jeremy James. 'It's cos of her legs.'

'Can't she get to the phone?'

Jeremy James called to Gran, but she didn't even move her head. Jeremy James told the lady again that Gran couldn't move, and so the lady asked him for Richard's address. Then she told him to stay with Gran, and to open the front door when the ambulance came.

'They're going to send an ampulus,' Jeremy James told Richard and Gran when he'd put the phone down.

Gran looked at him, and out of the corner of her mouth groaned something like 'Ickya'. She really was speaking a very strange language.

Five minutes later, a lot of things happened. An ambulance pah-pahed along the road and stopped at Richard's house, Jeremy James let the ambulance men in, Mr Biddles rushed round from next door, Jeremy James's mummy and some other neighbours arrived two minutes later, and everyone stood and watched as the ambulance men lifted Gran onto a stretcher and took her out.

'She's had a stroke,' one of the ambulance men told Mummy.

'*We* didn't stroke her!' said Jeremy James.

'A stroke's an illness,' Mummy explained. 'Gran's very ill, but you and Richard may have saved her life.'

While the ambulance drove Gran off to hospital, Mr Biddles rang Richard's mum and dad, and Mummy took Richard and Jeremy James home. Everyone agreed that they were both heroes for having put out the fire and sent for the ambulance.

It was not until some weeks later that Gran left hospital. She couldn't move one half of her body and she still talked in a funny way, out of the side of her mouth. But you could understand what she was saying now, and when Jeremy James went round to play with Richard again she said thank you to him.

'Clever lad,' she said. 'Just try not ter shut yerself in the lavat'ry.'

There had been two other big changes in Gran's life. The first was that she had stopped smoking.

'Silly habit, smokin',' she said. 'Smoke terday, ash termorrer.'

The other change was when she asked people to get things for her.

Before her illness, she'd always said: 'I can't move, yer see. It's becos of me legs.'

But now she said: 'I can't move, yer see. It's becos of me stroke.'

CHAPTER FOUR

Snap

If you had asked Jeremy James what he loved most in the world, he would probably have said Mummy and Daddy and the twins, chocolate and sweets and ice cream, and breakfast. Not necessarily in that order. What he disliked most was cabbage, nappy-smell, any sort of pain, and tea at Aunt Janet's.

The trouble with tea at Aunt Janet's wasn't the tea, and it wasn't Aunt Janet or Uncle Jack. The trouble was his cousin Melissa. She always wanted to play 'Freezing', in which one person hid things and the other person looked for them and Melissa always won. Jeremy James wasn't looking forward to this afternoon.

'I hope Melissa won't be scraping her violin!' said Daddy, as they drove through the pouring rain. Daddy wasn't looking forward to this afternoon either.

Jeremy James had hidden the violin in the goldfish pond one day, which had been the only time he'd ever beaten Melissa at 'Freezing'. Daddy had had to buy her a new one afterwards.

'Don't you go throwing her new one in the

goldfish pond,' said Daddy. 'Your bright ideas cost me a lot of money, Jeremy James.'

The rain was still pouring down when they reached Aunt Janet's house. Mummy carried Christopher, Daddy carried Jennifer, and Jeremy James offered to stay in the car till it was time to go home. But that was another bright idea that came to a wet conclusion.

'Oh, look at those adorable babies!' cried Aunt Janet, when Christopher and Jennifer had been unwrapped. 'My, haven't they grown! And Jeremy James too. You're a big boy, aren't you?'

Aunt Janet never talked about anything except how big everyone was, how tall everyone was, and how everyone had grown.

'They grow so fast, don't they?' she said to Mummy.

'Melissa's grown a lot too,' said Mummy, although Melissa was hiding behind Uncle Jack and could barely be seen.

'I know,' said Aunt Janet. 'In fact I think she's even taller than Jeremy James.'

Jeremy James stretched himself up to as tall as he could get.

'You may be right,' said Mummy.

'Let's see,' said Aunt Janet. 'Come here, darlings, and stand back to back.'

The pig-tailed Melissa, clutching her pig-tailed doll, emerged sulkily from behind Uncle Jack.

'Come on, Jeremy James,' said Aunt Janet, taking his arm. 'Just stand here, darling.'

Back to back with Melissa, Jeremy James tried to stretch himself up to even taller than he could get, but he couldn't get there.

'She is! She is!' cried Aunt Janet. 'Melissa wins!'

Jeremy James reckoned the afternoon would have been more enjoyable if he'd sat in the car watching the pouring rain.

'Now then, Jeremy James, dear,' said Aunt Janet, 'you go and play with Melissa, and we'll call you when tea's ready.'

Jeremy James reckoned the afternoon would have been more enjoyable if he'd sat in the car watching the pouring rain *and* had tummy ache.

Melissa, however, had a surprise in store. She did not want to play 'Freezing'. She wanted to play 'Snap'.

'What's "Snap"?' asked Jeremy James.

Melissa produced a pack of playing cards like the ones Mummy had taught him to play 'Patience' with. She explained that they must take turns in putting down a card, and if they both put down the same cards – like, say, nines or aces or jacks – they must shout 'Snap'. They mustn't shout before the cards were on the carpet, and whoever shouted first won the cards that had been put down. The winner would be the player who won all the cards.

It sounded simple. And it *was* simple. Each of them kept putting down their cards until Melissa shouted 'Snap', and then Jeremy James saw that there were two nines, or aces, or jacks on the carpet. No matter how quickly he looked at his own cards and Melissa's, she always shouted first. And when she took his last card, she shouted snap even before he'd seen what she was putting down.

'I won! I won!' cried Melissa. 'Let's play again!'

They played again, and Melissa won again. Not once did Jeremy James succeed in shouting snap before she did.

'It's because I'm very quick,' said Melissa. 'I've got wonderful eyes. Mummy says so.'

It was only during the third game that Jeremy James noticed something about Melissa's wonderful eyes. She was putting her cards down a little more slowly than he was, and was turning them towards herself, so that her wonderful eyes were able to see them before they were on the carpet. He'd been turning his own cards away from himself, and so her wonderful eyes saw those first too.

In the fourth game, things suddenly changed. Jeremy James shouted snap first and, sure enough, there were two sixes on the carpet.

'That's not fair,' said Melissa.

'Yes it is,' said Jeremy James. 'It's a six and a six.'

'You looked!' said Melissa.

'So did you,' said Jeremy James.

'You looked before you put the card down!' said Melissa.

'So did you,' said Jeremy James.

'Well I'm not playing any more,' said Melissa.

'Nor am I,' said Jeremy James.

It was one of the few occasions when Jeremy James and Melissa agreed.

'So I won,' said Melissa.

'No you didn't,' said Jeremy James.

It was one of the many occasions when Jeremy James and Melissa disagreed.

'I know a trick,' said Melissa.

'I don't care,' said Jeremy James.

'I'll bet you a bar of chocolate you don't know how it's done,' said Melissa.

Jeremy James did care. A bar of chocolate was worth caring about.

'All right,' he said, 'let's see your silly old trick.'

'What are you going to give me?' asked Melissa.

'What for?' asked Jeremy James.

'If you don't know how it's done,' replied Melissa.

Jeremy James didn't have a bar of chocolate, but Uncle Jack usually gave him some money when he left so he said he would give that to Melissa. She agreed,

134

gathered up all the cards, and put the pack face down on the carpet. Then she took off the top two cards, and told Jeremy James to look at the third card and remember what it was.

Jeremy James had a look at the card. It was the four of spades.

'Now put it back,' commanded Melissa.

Jeremy James put it back. Melissa then put the other two cards on top, and jumbled up the whole pack.

'I'm going to tell you which card it was,' said Melissa.

She turned the cards over one at a time and put them face up on the carpet. She had put down about twenty when she reached the four of spades.

'That's it,' she said. 'That was your card.'

'You saw!' said Jeremy James. 'You saw it when I picked it up!'

'No I didn't,' said Melissa.

'Well you saw when you jumbled up the cards!' said Jeremy James.

'No I didn't,' said Melissa.

'Do it again then!' said Jeremy James.

'All right,' said Melissa.

Jeremy James watched very carefully as she took off the top two cards. She definitely didn't look at the third one.

'Now look at that card,' she said.

Jeremy James slowly slid it off the pack, cupped it in his hand, glanced at it, then put it back. It was the queen of diamonds.

'You can put the other cards back too if you like,' said Melissa.

Jeremy James put the other cards back.

'And you can shuffle the cards yourself,' said Melissa.

Jeremy James shuffled the cards himself.

'Ready?' asked Melissa.

Jeremy James was ready. He gave her the cards, and one by one she turned them up. When she came to the queen of diamonds, she stopped.

'That's the card,' she said.

Jeremy James was baffled.

'You'll never guess how it's done!' said Melissa.

Jeremy James made her do the trick again – and again. And again. He turned his back on her, she turned her back on him, she left the room while he looked, *he* left the room while he looked – but somehow she always knew which card it was.

'Tea, children!' called Aunt Janet. 'Come along, dears!'

It was a really good tea, with scones and jam and cream, and strawberries and ice cream, and lemonade . . . But Jeremy James had his mind on other things. He kept looking at Melissa with a puzzled pout, and she kept looking at him with a smug smirk.

'Aren't they good children!' said Aunt Janet, as they gathered in the hall to say goodbye. 'Those adorable twins are so sweet. And they're growing so fast, I'm sure they've got taller since they arrived.'

At this moment Jeremy James was secretly

handing over to Melissa the pound which Uncle Jack had handed over to him two moments earlier.

'How did you do it?' he asked Melissa.

'Not telling!' said Melissa.

'Please!' pleaded Jeremy James.

'No!' said Melissa.

'And Melissa and Jeremy James get on so well together!' said Auntie Janet. 'You must come again soon.'

On the way back, Jeremy James told Mummy and Daddy about Melissa's trick, and Daddy laughed.

'I'll show you how it's done when we get home,' he said.

After Mummy and Daddy had bathed the twins and put them to bed, Daddy took out a pack of cards and he and Jeremy James sat at the dining room table.

'Now,' said Daddy, 'when you finished playing "Snap", Melissa must have had a look at the third card. So what's the third card here?'

It was the seven of hearts.

'So I know the third card is the seven of hearts, right? I take off the top two cards, you look at the third one . . . What is it?'

'The seven of hearts,' said Jeremy James.

'We put it back, shuffle all the cards – but I know it's the seven of hearts – and then I start to go through them one at a time looking for the seven of hearts. But as I go through them, I also look at the third card again and remember it for the next time. Here's the third card, which is . . . ?'

'The king of spades,' said Jeremy James.

137

'So I come to the seven of hearts . . . here it is . . . and you say wow, gosh, worple worple thaumaturgics, do it again, Daddy, do it again! Right?'

'Yes.'

'So I do it again. But now I know that the third card is . . . ?'

'The king of spades,' said Jeremy James.

'So you pick up the king of spades, put it back, shuffle the cards, and I start looking for the king of spades, but in the meantime I see the third card, which is . . . ?'

'The ace of clubs,' said Jeremy James.

'The ace of clubs. So I find the king of spades, and you say Daddy, you're a genius, how's it done? Do it again, and we do it again, and you pick up . . . '

'The ace of clubs,' said Jeremy James.

'And I could go on doing the same trick all night long,' said Daddy. 'Here, I'll teach you some more tricks, so you can get your own back on Melissa.'

By the time the lesson was over, Jeremy James had mastered half a dozen card tricks.

'Like most things,' said Daddy, 'it's simple when you know how to do it. Any questions?'

'Yes,' said Jeremy James. 'When can we go to Aunt Janet's again?'

CHAPTER FIVE

Mystery Smyth-Fortescue

Nobody knew what Mr Smyth-Fortescue did for a living. Daddy called him Mystery Smyth-Fortescue. He often went away to foreign countries, and would bring expensive presents back for his wife and for Timothy, like the wonderful thingummy from Switzerland. Mummy had once asked Mrs Smyth-Fortescue what her husband did.

'He's in business,' said Mrs Smyth-Fortescue.

'What sort of business?' asked Mummy.

'Big business,' said Mrs Smyth-Fortescue.

Roly-poly Richard, who was Jeremy James's best friend, reckoned he knew exactly what business Mr Smyth-Fortescue was in.

'He's a gangster!'

'How do you know?' asked Jeremy James.

'Cos I heard him talking about the underworld once,' said Richard, 'and that's where gangsters work. I know, cos I saw the underworld on telly. *And* he wears a hat.'

'My daddy sometimes wears a hat,' said Jeremy James.

'Mr Smyth-Fortescue's hat goes right down to

his eyes,' said Richard. 'That's what gangsters wear.'

'Do you think he's got a gun too?' asked Jeremy James.

'I bet he's got hundreds of guns,' said Richard. '*And* I bet they've got a cellar with dead bodies in it.'

'They *have* got a cellar,' said Jeremy James, 'cos Timothy went down there, and he wanted me to go with him!'

'I bet he'd have deaded you!' said Richard. 'And buried you with all the other dead bodies.'

The two boys were playing in Jeremy James's room, and the reason why they were talking about the Smyth-Fortescues was that everybody always talked about the Smyth-Fortescues.

'What we need to do,' said Richard, 'is find the guns and the dead bodies and tell the police.'

'I could tell the police that Timothy wanted to dead me with his thingummy from Sweaterland,' said Jeremy James.

'The police like to have real dead bodies,' said Richard. 'I've seen it on telly.'

'Well I don't want to be a real dead body,' said Jeremy James. 'Specially not a real dead body deaded by Timothy.'

It was at that moment that there was a ring at the doorbell, and soon afterwards Mummy's voice came up the stairs:

'Jeremy James, it's Timothy! Do you and Richard want to go and play at his house?'

141

Jeremy James looked at Richard, and Richard looked at Jeremy James. This could be their chance.

'One of us can play with him,' whispered Jeremy James, 'while the other looks for the dead bodies.'

'All right,' whispered Richard. 'I'll play with him, and you can look for the dead bodies.'

Mummy was quite surprised at how enthusiastically they agreed to play with Timothy. Jeremy James usually said he was too busy working, resting, or worple-worpling.

'Is your daddy at home?' Jeremy James asked Timothy as they all went next door.

'No,' said Timothy, 'he's gone to America.'

'He's always going to America,' said Richard.

'That's cos his boss is there,' said Timothy.

Jeremy James and Richard exchanged knowing looks.

'The boss is called the Godfather,' whispered Richard. 'I saw it on the telly.'

The next stroke of luck came when Mrs Smyth-Fortescue popped her head round Timothy's door to say she was going to sit out in the garden. 'Just call me if you need anything,' she said.

'I need some chocolate,' said Timothy.

'There'll be chocolate for the *good* children later!' said Mrs Smyth-Fortescue with a smile. 'And Timothy will tell me who's been good, won't you, dear?'

'I want fruit and nut,' said Timothy.

Mrs Smyth-Fortescue left them all playing a computer game which Timothy was bound to win

142

because Timothy only played games which he was bound to win. After a few minutes, Jeremy James stood up.

'I've got to go to the lavatory,' he announced, with another knowing look at Richard, who gave him another knowing look back.

'That's cos you're losing,' said Timothy.

'No it isn't,' said Jeremy James. 'It's cos I've got a tummy ache, and I might be gone for a little while cos it's a big tummy ache.'

'Well you've lost then,' said Timothy.

'I don't care,' said Jeremy James, 'cos I've got tummy ache.'

'Only little kids get tummy ache when they're losing,' said Timothy.

'I haven't got tummy ache,' said Richard, 'so I'm still playing.'

'But I'm winning,' said Timothy. 'I always win.'

Jeremy James closed the door behind him, and began the hunt for gangsters, guns and dead bodies. It was exciting, but it was also dangerous. Gangsters, guns and dead bodies might be anywhere. He carefully opened the first door, and found himself looking into a gangsterless, gunless, bodiless bedroom with two beds, mirrors, wardrobes and a dressing-table. The bathroom, another bedroom, separate lavatory, and a room full of computers and files all turned out to be as exciting and dangerous as a baby having a good night's sleep.

However, all the best detectives know that dead bodies are kept in cellars, and so Jeremy James made his way downstairs to the kitchen. And there he waited, trembling, outside the cellar door.

This was really dangerous. Really, *really* dangerous. Supposing he opened the door and a dead body fell on him? Or a gangster fired a gun at him? Then *he* would become a dead body, and he would never be seen again. Mummy would come and call him for tea, and he wouldn't be there. And he wouldn't get his tea either.

Jeremy James decided not to open the cellar door. There were more important things in life than dead bodies. Live bodies, for instance. And tea.

On the other hand, if he didn't open the cellar door, they would never know the truth about Mr Smyth-Fortescue. And what would he tell Richard, who was up in Timothy's room at this moment imagining Jeremy James down in the cellar at this moment?

The cellar door had to be opened.

With his hand shaking, and his heart banging in his chest, Jeremy James opened the cellar door. There was a light switch on the wall, and a steep flight of steps leading downwards. He turned on the light.

'Is anybody there?' called Jeremy James.

Not a sound.

Slowly he eased his way down the steps, one at a time.

The cellar was huge, and the light was dim. There were wine racks along one wall, with lots and lots of bottles, but no guns and no bodies. Along another wall there were boxes – lots and lots of boxes, stacked

in neat piles. You could keep guns in boxes like those. Lots and lots of guns. There was some old furniture too, and . . . and . . . what was that in the far corner?

Jeremy James stood very still, very quiet, very pale, and very frightened.

Over in the shadows of that far corner, standing, sitting, lying down, there were people. Lots and lots of people. Lots and lots of dead people.

'He–he–hello!' he gulped.

They didn't answer.

'Are . . . are you all right?'

They didn't move.

'Are . . . are you dead?'

They didn't say yes. They didn't say no. Dead people don't say anything. Jeremy James unparalysed himself and ran up the cellar steps like a boy who had just seen a dozen ghosts.

The telephone was in the hall. For a moment he hesitated. Maybe he should tell Daddy first. But no, Daddy would just look at the dead bodies and say, 'There's nothing we can do'. This was a matter for the police.

Jeremy James dialled 999.

A lot of things happened during the next ten minutes. First, Jeremy James rushed up to Timothy's room to warn Richard.

'They're in the cellar!' he cried.

Richard turned pale.

'What's in the cellar?' asked Timothy.

'All the dead bodies!' cried Jeremy James. 'Come on, Richard, we've got to let the police in!'

Next the police arrived – three of them, led by a man with bushy eyebrows – and hardly had Jeremy James shown them the way to the cellar door when Mummy and Daddy arrived too. They'd heard the police siren.

'What's going on?' asked Daddy.

'Leave it to us, sir!' said the bushy policeman. 'Stand clear.'

He pulled open the cellar door, and he and his men thundered down the cellar steps.

'What's going on, Jeremy James?' asked Daddy.

Jeremy James quickly explained that Mr Smyth-Fortescue was a gangster, and there were dead bodies in the cellar.

A few moments later, the policemen came back up the cellar steps and out into the kitchen.

'Did you find anything, Officer?' asked Daddy.

'Are you the owner of this 'ere establishment, sir?' asked the bushy policeman.

'No,' said Daddy.

'Then where *is* the owner?'

'She's out in the garden,' said Jeremy James.

Then the policemen, followed by Mummy and Daddy, Richard and Jeremy James, all trooped into the garden, where Mrs Smyth-Fortescue was fast asleep in a deckchair under the apple tree.

'Wake up, madam,' said the bushy policeman, shaking her shoulder.

'Oh, good heavens!' cried Mrs Smyth-Fortescue. 'What's happened? Timothy! Where's my Timothy?'

Indeed there was no sign of Timothy.

'I bet he's escaped!' Richard whispered to Jeremy James. 'That's what gangsters do when the police are onto them. They go to the underworld. I've seen it on telly.'

'Calm down, madam,' said the bushy policeman. 'Are you the owner of this establishment?'

'Yes, yes!' cried Mrs Smyth-Fortescue. 'Tell me what's happened!'

'We received a telephone call,' said the policeman, 'informin' us that there was a lot of dead bodies in your cellar.'

'Dead bodies!' shrieked Mrs Smyth-Fortescue.

'We 'ave now investigated your cellar, madam,' the policeman went on, 'and 'ave found a number of shop dummies, plus 'undreds o' boxes of underwear. Women's and men's.'

147

'They're my husband's,' said Mrs Smyth-Fortescue. 'That's his business.'

'An' a very important business it is too, madam,' said the policeman. 'Close to all our 'earts. Now I'd like to know if there's a Jeremy James 'ere.'

There *was* a Jeremy James there. And the bushy policeman had quite a lot to say to Jeremy James, as well as to Jeremy James's mummy and daddy. Most of what he had to say concerned the difference between dead bodies and shop dummies, the wastage of police time, and the importance of parents keeping their children under control.

'Although I must admit,' said the policeman, 'that just for a moment I did think we was onto something. Them dummies can be very lifelike. Or even deadlike.'

When the police had left, Mummy and Daddy also had quite a lot to say to Jeremy James, and Jeremy James had to say sorry to Mrs Smyth-Fortescue, and Mrs Smyth-Fortescue said it was all right, but where was her darling, precious Timothy?

It turned out that Timothy hadn't escaped after all. He was sitting in his room, at his computer.

'*There* you are, darling!' cried Mrs Smyth-Fortescue. 'Thank Heaven you're safe!'

'I won,' announced Timothy. 'And where's my chocolate?'

Later, at tea, Mummy and Daddy were talking about the Smyth-Fortescues.

'I suppose he could have been a gangster,' said Mummy. 'You can never be sure about people.'

'He could still be a gangster,' said Daddy. 'Underwear can be a cover for some pretty nasty things.'

'I don't think he is a gangster, though,' said Jeremy James.

'Why not?' asked Daddy.

'Cos Richard made a mistake,' said Jeremy James. 'He thought Mr Smyth-Fortyshoe was talking about the underworld, but he must have been talking about the underwear.'

And so the mystery of Mr Smyth-Fortescue was finally solved.

CHAPTER SIX

The Boot Sale

Mummy wanted to go to a car boot sale. Daddy wanted to 'do some work', but Mummy said it was a lovely afternoon, she could do with an outing, and Daddy could watch recorded highlights in the evening.

Jeremy James didn't know that cars wore boots, and so Mummy explained that the boot was the back of the car, where people put their luggage.

'Why does Daddy want to sell the back of the car?' asked Jeremy James. After all, it was the front of the car that usually caused the trouble.

Mummy said they weren't going to sell *any* of the car. A boot sale was where people put things in the back of their cars and took them to a kind of market to sell them. There might also be an ice cream van there and a bouncy castle.

Mummy and Daddy strapped Jeremy James and the twins into their seats, and put the twins' pram in the boot.

'Why are we selling the pram?' asked Jeremy James, but Mummy said they were *not* selling the pram.

'But it's in the boot,' said Jeremy James.

'We're not selling,' explained Mummy. 'We're buying.'

Jeremy James thought they'd already bought the pram, and Mummy said they *had* bought the pram. It was all very confusing.

On the way they stopped behind a blue car, and peeping out of its back window was a brown dog with big round eyes.

'Can we buy the dog?' asked Jeremy James.

'The dog's not for sale,' said Daddy.

Jeremy James gave up trying to understand car boot sales – and grown-ups.

The sale was being held in a large field, and when they had parked the car, they walked across to where the crowds were. There were hundreds of cars and thousands of people with millions of things spread out on stands and tables and even on the ground.

'Bargain of the century!' someone shouted, and elsewhere voices were crying: 'Lovely and fresh!' and 'Everything must go!' and 'Only the best!'

There were pictures and clothes and shoes and furniture and records and tapes and tools and flowers and necklaces and earrings . . .

'Ah!' said Mummy. 'Necklaces and earrings.'

Mummy spent quite a long time looking at necklaces and earrings, and finally bought a pair of earrings which looked just like the earrings she was wearing but only cost a pound.

. . . And meat and fish and soap and toothpaste

and saucepans and plates and cups and saucers and books . . .

'Ah!' said Daddy. 'Books.'

Daddy spent even longer looking at books than Mummy had spent looking at earrings, and he finally bought a book which looked just like the other books in his study but only cost fifty pence.

. . . And curtains and carpets and sheets and cushions and telephones and radios and TV sets and lamps and toys and games . . .

'Ah!' said Jeremy James. 'Toys and games.'

'Come on, Jeremy James,' said Mummy. 'We can't spend all day looking at toys and games.'

Jeremy James could have spent several days looking at toys and games, and toys and games were a lot more interesting than earrings and necklaces and books and . . .

'There's the ice cream van,' said Daddy.

'Ah!' said Jeremy James.

The car boot sale was a great success. Jeremy James got a game, a toy lorry and a packet of sweets, *and* he had a bounce on the bouncy castle; Mummy bought some more earrings and a bracelet and some magazines and a shawl and some flowers and some bananas and a useful whatsit; Daddy bought some more books and a magnifying glass (he wanted to look at his hair); Christopher got a cuddly bear, and Jennifer got a doll which said 'Mama' and which she named Carboo.

Jeremy James enjoyed buying things. He especially enjoyed buying things like toys and games and sweets and chocolate. He could have gone on buying toys and games and sweets and chocolate all day long. However, experience had taught Jeremy James that in order to buy things you needed money, and money was something he had very little of. He had tried to get a job once, delivering goods for the greengrocer, but a little boy who was saving up for a tricycle was not quite what the greengrocer had been looking for.

The car boot sale, however, had given Jeremy James an idea. He didn't have his own car, of course, but Daddy's car would be nearby, and nobody would know that it wasn't Jeremy James's.

He explained his idea to Mummy and Daddy, and they laughed but said it was all right and he could go ahead. Daddy even wrote a big notice for him. The notice said:

GIANT CAR BOOT SALE
HERE TODAY
Entrance 5p

Jeremy James had wanted to charge fifty pence entrance, but Daddy didn't think anyone would pay that much for a one-car boot sale, even if it was a giant one-car boot sale.

Jeremy James spread all his old books and toys and games out on the front lawn, together with some clothes and books Daddy gave him, and some clothes and pots and earrings Mummy gave him, and then he stood by the front gate to wait for his customers.

The first customer was old Mrs Dingle, who was

on her way home from the supermarket. She had her head down as she pulled her trolley, and so she didn't see the notice.

'Everything must go!' cried Jeremy James. 'Bargain of the century!'

Mrs Dingle looked up and stopped.

'Oh!' she said. 'What are you selling?'

'It's five pence to enter,' said Jeremy James.

'I can see what you've got from here,' said Mrs Dingle, peering over the garden gate. 'And I don't think there's anything for me there. But you take this and see if you can sell it.'

From her trolley she pulled out a small bar of chocolate, which she handed to Jeremy James over the garden gate.

'Thank you very much!' said Jeremy James, and the old lady smiled and went on her way.

Jeremy James decided not to sell the bar of chocolate. Bars of chocolate were for buying and eating, not for selling.

The next customer came in a van which stopped right outside the house. Out got a man in a peaked cap, and he walked straight to the front gate. Jeremy James reckoned the man would have room in his van for all the goods, and so he began to wonder how much he should ask for if the man wanted to buy everything.

'Hello,' said the man.

'Hello,' said Jeremy James. 'Five pence, please.'

'Five pence?' said the man.

'To come in,' said Jeremy James.

'Oh!' said the man, spotting the notice and then the collection of treasures. 'A sale, eh? Well, I've only come to read your electricity meter.'

The man opened the gate himself, and walked round the side of the house. He was gone for a minute or two, then came back with his notebook in his hand.

'That's it,' he said. 'Thanks very much.'

Then he opened the garden gate, got into his van, and drove away.

The milkman was the next customer.

'Giant car boot?' said the milkman. 'Where's the giant car then?'

'There isn't a giant car,' said Jeremy James. 'There's a giant sale.'

'I don't want to buy a giant,' said the milkman.

Jeremy James explained that he wasn't selling giants, he was just selling the things on the front lawn. To his surprise, the milkman gave him five pence, and then to his even greater surprise, the milkman gave him fifty pence for one of Daddy's old books.

'Our kitchen table's got a short leg,' he said, 'and this'll do just right.'

When the milkman had gone, business went quiet for a little while, until there emerged from next door the familiar figures of Mrs Smyth-Fortescue and the red-haired Timothy.

'Hello, Jeremy dear,' said Mrs Smyth-Fortescue. 'What's this? A car boot sale?'

'It's five pence to enter,' said Jeremy James.

'I'm afraid we never buy used goods,' said Mrs Smyth-Fortescue. 'One never knows where they've been.'

'They've been here,' said Jeremy James.

'Ah!' said Mrs Smyth-Fortescue.

'Who wants your old junk?' scoffed Timothy.

'Lots of people,' said Jeremy James. '*And* a lady gave me a bar of chocolate.'

He pulled the chocolate out of his pocket and waved it in the air. Timothy's eyes were filled with a chocolate-wanting gleam.

'How much is it?' he asked.

'A hundred pounds,' said Jeremy James.

Timothy looked at his mother.

'I want it,' he said.

'I think a hundred pounds is a little expensive, dear,' said Mrs Smyth-Fortescue to Jeremy James. 'But I'll give you twenty pence.'

She held out twenty pence, and Timothy held out his hand, and Jeremy James looked at the twenty pence and looked at Timothy's hand and looked at the chocolate.

'The chocolate's not for sale,' he announced, and put it back in his pocket.

'Thirty pence then,' said Mrs Smyth-Fortescue, but Jeremy James would not have accepted even a hundred pounds now – well, perhaps a hundred pounds, but definitely not thirty pence.

'Come along, Timothy,' said Mrs Smyth-Fortescue. 'I'll buy you one at the supermarket.'

'I want that one,' said Timothy.

But Mrs Smyth-Fortescue was already on her way. Timothy poked his tongue out at Jeremy James as he followed his mother down the street, but Jeremy James did nothing so childish. He simply pulled the chocolate out of his pocket again, unwrapped it, and watched Timothy's face as he bit off two squares. Timothy did not look happy.

A few more customers came and went. Mostly they were people who lived in the street. Richard came, but he didn't have any money, and so Jeremy James let him in for nothing and told him to take whatever he liked. Richard took a book for Gran and an old saucepan that might come in useful one day.

Little Trevor, who lived round the corner, only had five pence, which was a bit of a problem. If he paid five pence to come in, he wouldn't be able to buy anything, but if he didn't come in he wouldn't be able to buy anything either. In the end, Jeremy James let him in for nothing, but then he didn't want to buy anything so he went away with his five pence still in his pocket.

The last customer was a policeman. He came riding by on his bike, saw the notice, got off his bike, and came to the garden gate.

'Lovely and fresh!' cried Jeremy James. 'Only the best!'

'So what's goin' on 'ere, then?' asked the policeman.

'It's a giant car boot sale,' said Jeremy James, 'and it costs five pence to come in.'

'Do it now?' said the policeman. 'An' might I ask if you got a licence ter run a car boot sale?'

'What's a licence?' asked Jeremy James.

'A licence,' said the policeman, 'is a permit. You 'as ter get a permit.'

'What's a permit?' asked Jeremy James.

'A permit,' said the policeman, 'is a licence. You can't 'old a boot sale unless you 'as a licence. Or a permit.'

'Well, it's a giant boot sale,' said Jeremy James.

'In that case,' said the policeman, 'you 'as to 'ave a giant licence or permit.'

Jeremy James still didn't know what a licence or permit was, but whatever it was, he didn't think he had one.

'I've got a bar of chocolate,' he said. 'Or a bit of one. Will that do?'

At this moment, Daddy came out of the front door.

'Afternoon, Officer,' he said. 'Anything the matter?'

'Afternoon, sir,' said the policeman. 'I 'as ter tell you, sir, that no one's allowed to 'old a car boot sale without a licence.'

'Oh!' said Daddy. 'Well actually, it's not a *real* car boot sale.'

'It might not look like a real car boot sale, sir, but a sale is a sale an' the law is the law, an' the law says you 'as to 'ave a licence.'

'Oh dear,' said Daddy. 'Then we'd better pack up, Jeremy James.'

'Well before you do, sir, them there earrings, 'ow much would they be?'

'Fifty pence.'

'A pound.'

(That was Daddy and Jeremy James speaking at the same time.)

'Seventy-five pence?' suggested the policeman.

Daddy and Jeremy James both said yes, and the policeman gave Jeremy James a pound and told him to keep the change.

'Just the sort o' earrings me wife likes,' said the policeman. 'Glad I came by.'

The policeman cycled off, and Daddy and Jeremy James closed the Giant Car Boot Sale, even though most of the lovely, fresh bargains of the century had not yet been sold.

When Daddy counted up all the money, it came to a grand total of four pounds and fifty-five pence.

160

'And what are you going to do with all that?' asked Mummy.

Jeremy James looked at her in surprise.

'Spend it at the next car boot sale,' he said.

CHAPTER SEVEN

Charity

The day after Jeremy James's boot sale, Mummy and Daddy were talking about something called the 'developing world'. They were saying how unfair it was that people in the West had more than they needed, while people in the developing world didn't have enough.

Jeremy James certainly didn't have enough money or chocolate or liquorice all-sorts. If people in the West had more money, chocolate and liquorice all-sorts than they needed, maybe they would give some to him.

'Can we go to the West?' he asked.

'We're *in* the West,' said Daddy.

'Have we got more than we need, then?' asked Jeremy James.

'Well, generally, yes,' said Daddy.

'So can I have some?' asked Jeremy James.

'Some what?' asked Mummy.

Jeremy James went through his little list, but what he needed was not what people in the developing world needed. A lot of them didn't have food or clothes or homes.

'There are children like you,' said Daddy, 'who are starving. You're not starving, are you?'

Actually, Jeremy James *was* starving. Breakfast had been four hours ago, and he was ready for his lunch.

'Well, a lot of people in the developing world are ready for their lunch,' said Daddy, 'but they won't get it. And they may not even have had breakfast.'

'Haven't people in the developing world got mummies and daddies, then?' asked Jeremy James.

Daddy said they did have mummies and daddies, but the mummies and daddies didn't have enough to eat either.

That morning, Jeremy James did some deep and serious thinking. If people were not getting enough to eat, they must be very hungry. They probably wouldn't even mind what they ate. And if they didn't mind what they ate, maybe he could help them.

Mummy was in the kitchen, cooking, when Jeremy James came in with his solution to the problems of the developing world.

'What have we got for lunch?' he asked.

'We've got chicken, boiled potatoes, carrots and Brussel sprouts,' said Mummy, 'followed by raspberry jelly and ice cream.'

Jeremy James did a little more thinking.

'Well,' he said, 'if I had the chicken and the raspberry jelly and the ice cream, you could give the potatoes and carrots and bustle spouts to the developing world.'

Mummy laughed.

163

'Well, yes, I could, but by the time they got it all, it would have gone bad. And besides, Jeremy James, they'd need millions and millions of potatoes and stuff to feed them.'

'Well they can have *all* my potatoes and stuff,' said Jeremy James. 'And . . . and I suppose they could have my chicken too.'

Mummy said it was a wonderful idea, and if everybody in England did that, it really would help. But on the other hand, Jeremy James must also have enough to eat, or he would end up getting just as thin as the people in the developing world.

'Well, I could have some extra jelly and ice cream,' said Jeremy James.

'Hmmph!' said Mummy.

If Jeremy James had suggested eating more potatoes and stuff, and sending away his jelly and ice cream, she'd probably have said yes. But Jeremy James didn't suggest it. There were limits to what even he could do for the developing world. Instead he had a new idea.

'How far away is the developing world?' he asked.

'Thousands of miles,' said Mummy.

'Could I take my potatoes and stuff there on my tricycle?'

'Yes, but you wouldn't get there until you were about Daddy's age.'

Jeremy James gave up his new idea.

He was very quiet all through lunch, apart from the noise he made while munching his chicken and potatoes and stuff. His mind was on other things – in particular raspberry jelly and ice cream. However, when he had had his raspberry jelly and ice cream, his mind turned once more to the developing world.

'Why can't the developing world people come here?' he asked.

Daddy explained that there were millions of them, and even if they could travel, there just wouldn't be room for them.

'I'm afraid there's nothing you or I can do, Jeremy James,' said Daddy. 'So have a second helping of jelly and ice cream.'

Jeremy James had his second helping. Refusing a second helping would not have fed the developing world, and it would also have left an empty space in his stomach which he had specially reserved for second helpings.

Nevertheless, Jeremy James was sure that he *could* do something, and so while Daddy was working in his study, and Mummy was out for a walk with the twins, he sat up in his room thinking. And what he was thinking was this:

You can't send your potatoes and stuff to the developing world, and the developing world can't come to you. But how do you get potatoes and stuff (not to mention raspberry jelly and ice cream) in the first place? Well, you go to the supermarket and buy them. That's what Mummy did. Why, then, couldn't the developing world go to the supermarket and buy food?

'Because they haven't got any money!' said Jeremy James aloud.

He had solved the problem. Almost.

The 'almost' bit was that he still needed help, but he knew just the person who could help him. Mr Drew was the kind, grey-haired man who ran the sweet shop. He also sold cigarettes and birthday cards and sticky tape and pens and pencils . . . Mr Drew would know what to do.

Jeremy James hurried downstairs to Daddy's study.

'Please can I go to the sweet shop?' he asked.

'OK,' said Daddy, 'but nowhere else, and don't go into the road.'

Jeremy James rushed upstairs again, grabbed his money-box, rushed downstairs, jumped onto his tricycle, and with legs spinning like propellers went racing up the road and round the corner to Mr Drew's.

'Hello, Jeremy James,' said Mr Drew. 'What's it to be? Fruit and nut today?'

'No, thank you, Mr Drew,' said Jeremy James.

'Ah, it's a liquorice all-sort day, is it?'

'No,' said Jeremy James. 'I'd like an envelope, please.'

'An envelope? How big?'

'It's to put this in.'

Jeremy James opened his money-box. Inside were a lot of jingling coins – four pounds and fifty-five pence to be precise.

'My word, that's a lot of money,' said Mr Drew. 'And you want to put it in an envelope, do you?'

'Yes, please,' said Jeremy James.

Mr Drew thought the money-box was a much better place for it than an envelope, but if the customer wanted an envelope, then an envelope he would have.

'One of these thick, padded ones would be best,' said Mr Drew. He opened the envelope, and Jeremy James poured the coins inside.

'So what are you going to do with all that money, Jeremy James?' asked Mr Drew.

'Send it,' said Jeremy James. 'Please would you write "The Developing World" on it?'

'The Developing World?'

'That's where I'm sending it to.'

Jeremy James told Mr Drew all about the developing world, and how he was going to help them.

'This is the money I got from the car boot sale, so the developing world can go to the supermarket and buy jelly and ice cream. Or potatoes and stuff.'

Mr Drew didn't say anything for a moment. He nodded, and blinked, and then he smiled.

'Could I make a suggestion?' he asked. 'The developing world is a very, very big place. There's no telling where this envelope could end up, and somebody on the way might even steal the money. So my suggestion is that you take it home, and ask your dad to give it to charity. Do you know what charity is?'

Jeremy James didn't know.

'Your dad'll tell you,' said Mr Drew.

'Daddy doesn't know very much,' said Jeremy James. 'He didn't know that we could help the developing world.'

'He'll know about charity,' said Mr Drew. 'And that way, your money will arrive safely. Now, can I make two more suggestions?'

Jeremy James nodded.

'One is that I give you another forty-five pence, to make this up to five pounds. And the other is that you take this bar of fruit and nut as a little present from a member of the developed world.'

Jeremy James thought these were both very good suggestions.

Mummy had just come back with the twins when Jeremy James arrived home and announced that he was going to give his money to charity. Mummy said that was a wonderful idea, and Daddy said that was a big word, and Jeremy James asked what it meant.

'Charities are organizations that help sick or poor people,' said Mummy.

'How do you know about charities?' asked Daddy.

Jeremy James told them all about his plan, and about Mr Drew's suggestions.

'I thought you wanted to spend the money at a car boot sale,' said Mummy.

'I did,' said Jeremy James, 'but I don't *need* to.'

All that remained was to choose the charity, and Jeremy James said it had to be one that helped the developing world.

'Well, there's Unicef, Oxfam, Save the Children . . .'

'Save the Children!' said Jeremy James.

And so it was decided that Jeremy James's five pounds, plus an additional five pounds from Daddy, should be sent to Save the Children. Daddy took Jeremy James's money, and wrote out a cheque, and he also wrote a letter to go with the cheque. The letter said:

To Save the Children

My name is Jeremy James,
    And I'm only very small.
I haven't got much money,
    But you can have it all.

Please save the developing world children –
    As many as you can –
And I'll try to send you more
    When I grow up to be a man.

Two weeks later, a letter arrived addressed to
Jeremy James. It was from Save the Children, and it
read as follows:

To Jeremy James

Thank you for the money.
    We'll save all the lives we can,
And we think that you've already
    Grown up to be a man.

Jeremy James didn't quite understand the letter,
but Mummy and Daddy said they agreed – and so
did Mr Drew.

CHAPTER EIGHT

Swimming

'Don't you think he's a bit young?' said Mummy.

'You're never too young to learn,' said Daddy.

They were talking about swimming lessons for Jeremy James. A little while ago he'd been fishing with Daddy, and had fallen into the water. Daddy had jumped in and saved him, and Daddy thought it might be better if he learnt how to save himself.

'Young Timothy next door is going to have lessons,' said Daddy. 'Though knowing him, he'll probably be teaching the instructor.'

'Do you want to go too?' Mummy asked Jeremy James.

Jeremy James did want to go. He didn't want Timothy to do something he couldn't do.

As it happened, the first lesson was on a Tuesday afternoon, and Daddy had to be away. Mrs Smyth-Fortescue therefore kindly offered to take 'dear Jeremy' along with 'dear Timothy', and to bring them back afterwards.

'Swimming's easy,' said Timothy, as they sat in the back of Mrs Smyth-Fortescue's car. 'I can swim hundreds of miles already.'

171

'Then why do you need lessons?' asked Jeremy James.

'Just in case,' said Timothy.

'Just in case what?' asked Jeremy James.

'Just in case of drownedings,' said Timothy.

'What are drownedings?' asked Jeremy James.

'Drownedings are when people like you can't swim.'

Jeremy James remembered something that had happened in Warkin-on-Sea. Timothy had gone beyond a red flag and had got caught by the tide, so Daddy had had to rush into the sea to rescue him.

'He didn't have to rescue me,' said Timothy. 'I could have swimmed all the way home if I'd wanted.'

'Swum, dear,' said Mrs Smyth-Fortescue over her shoulder. 'Not swimmed. And you mustn't tell fibs.'

'I'm not telling fibs!' cried Timothy. 'I can swim like a dish.'

'A fish, dear.'

'I can swim like a dish *and* a fish.'

The swimming instructor was a young black man, and he had the biggest muscles Jeremy James had ever seen. Each of his arms was like a snake that's swallowed a cannonball.

'How do you get such big muscles?' asked Jeremy James.

'Swimmin',' said the instructor. 'If you learn to swim, you'll get a body jus' like mine.'

Jeremy James couldn't wait to be a swimmer.

There were twelve children altogether, but Jeremy

James didn't know any of the others. The instructor, whose name was Mr Ambrose, made them all put on armbands, and then he called out in a sing-song voice, which echoed all round the swimming pool:

'Into the water you must go,
Down the steps, kids, nice 'n' slow.'

The children followed one another down the steps into the blue water, which came right up to Jeremy James's chest.

'The water smells funny,' Jeremy James said to Timothy.

'That's because it's got comicals in it,' said Timothy.

'How's the water?' shouted Mr Ambrose.

One of the children said it was wet, but the others shouted back that it was cold.

'Then hold your nose an' shut your eyes
An' duck your head for a nice surprise.'

Jeremy James held his nose, shut his eyes, ducked his head, and had a shock. Not only were his ears full of water, but he'd also forgotten to close his mouth, and so that was full of water too. He just had time to spit it out when the next order came:

'Now have a splash an' jump aroun',
An' get your two feet off the groun'.'

The children all jumped around and laughed, and Timothy splashed Jeremy James, so Jeremy James splashed Timothy, and some water went into Timothy's eye and he said 'Ouch!' and 'Stop it!'

'Now you're doin' what you oughter.
Don't be scared of a drop o' water!'

173

After a minute or two of this, Mr Ambrose sang:
'Now stan' still with feet on the bottom,
An' hol' your arms just like I got 'em.'
He moved his arms ahead and then to the sides, and all the children except Timothy did the same. Timothy was still wiping the water out of his eye.

'Y'all right there, Timothy?' asked Mr Ambrose.

'Jeremy James splashed water in my eye,' complained Timothy.

'Then look out the other eye,' said Mr Ambrose.

Now the children were told to come to the side, and hold onto the bar which went all round the pool:
'Hold the bar, an' for the next trick,
Lift your legs an' give a kick.'
Jeremy James held onto the bar, and let his legs go up. They floated out behind him, and so he gave a mighty kick.

'That's the way, Jeremy James, you kick that water right out the other side o' the pool!'

All the children (except Timothy) were thoroughly enjoying themselves, and even the mums and dads up in the spectators' gallery were laughing away. Learning to swim was fun, especially when Mr Ambrose sang out his orders.

'Now take two steps away from the bar –
Not too near, an' not too far.
Jump an' kick, reach out your hand
An' grab the bar. Now ain't that grand?'
'That's not swimming,' hissed Timothy to Jeremy James. 'Swimming people don't wear armbands, and

they swim up and down the pool. I've seen them on TV.'

'Well, we're only *learning* to swim,' said Jeremy James.

'I'm not,' said Timothy. 'I can swim already. This is just for little kids like you.'

Mr Ambrose had them doing a lot more exercises and movements, and it seemed as if the lesson had hardly begun when he said:

'That's your first lesson at the swimmin' school,
So now come slowly out o' the pool.'

One by one the children came up the steps, and Mr Ambrose took each of them by the hand to help them out. Then he told them to take off their armbands, and called to the mums and dads to go down to the changing rooms. There was a little round of applause, because everyone had enjoyed the lesson so much.

Everyone, that is, except Timothy. He was now telling another boy called Geoffrey that the lesson had been 'kids' stuff', and the armbands were silly, and real swimmers like him could swim hundreds of miles without them.

'You c'n swim 'undreds o' miles, can you?' said Geoffrey.

'Of course I can,' said Timothy.

Different people gave different accounts of what happened next, though everyone agreed on what happened after what happened next. The *after* bit was that there was a loud cry, and Timothy fell into the water. He made a big splash and then went straight down to the bottom of the pool. Mr Ambrose raced along the side, dived in, swooped to the bottom, and in no time had lifted Timothy back up to the surface. Timothy was howling and spluttering as Mr Ambrose hoisted him up onto dry land and then hoisted himself up.

It took several minutes for Timothy to finish howling, by which time Mrs Smyth-Fortescue had joined the crowd at the side of the pool.

'He's all right,' said Mr Ambrose. 'It's jus' the shock. Nothin' wrong with him.'

'Thank you for saving him,' said Mrs Smyth-Fortescue, picking up her sobbing son. 'There, there, darling. Don't cry. Mummy's here.'

The different versions of what happened *before* the *after* bit were as follows:

177

Timothy: That boy . . . sob sob . . . pushed me.

Geoffrey: I never done nuffin'.

Geoffrey's mum: My boy never done nuffin'.

A boy called John: He fell in the water.

Timothy: I didn't . . . sob sob . . . He pushed me.

Geoffrey: I never touched 'im.

Geoffrey's mum: My boy never touched 'im.

Mrs Smyth-Fortescue: I'm sure it was just an accident.

Timothy: No it . . . sob sob . . . wasn't.

Mr Ambrose: He's all right, so ev'rybody can go home now.

Timothy: Sob sob.

Mrs Smyth-Fortescue: There there, darling.

Geoffrey: Anyway, 'e said 'e could swim.

Jeremy James had seen (and heard) exactly what had happened, but nobody asked him and so he didn't say anything. It was only when he got home that he told Mummy and Daddy all about it.

'And did Geoffrey push Timothy?' asked Mummy.

'Yes,' said Jeremy James. 'But I *thought* of pushing him.'

'Why didn't you?' asked Daddy.

'In case of drownedings,' said Jeremy James.

It took Jeremy James just three weeks to learn how to swim without armbands, and within a couple more weeks everyone else in the class had learned as well. Everyone except Timothy. His first lesson had been his last. After all, if you can swim hundreds of miles, what do you need swimming lessons for?

178

CHAPTER NINE

The Lion

There were some new neighbours. They weren't next-door neighbours like the Smyth-Fortescues, but lived down the road, on the way to the supermarket and the sweet shop. There were three of them altogether, but at first Jeremy James only saw one. It was while he was on his way to the sweet shop. Just as he rode past a house with a high hedge, there was a 'WOOF!' which was so loud that the sound waves nearly knocked him off his tricycle. Standing at the garden gate, with its nose poking over the top, was . . .

'A lion!' cried Jeremy James, and pedalled away so fast that his legs looked like circles.

When Jeremy James told Mr Drew the sweet shop man about the lion, Mr Drew laughed.

'That's not a lion,' he said, 'it's a big dog. Have another look when you go past.'

Jeremy James would have liked to go past on the other side of the street, but he wasn't allowed to cross the road, so he slowed down and went right to the edge of the pavement.

'WOOF!' roared the monster as Jeremy James came near, and again the great nose poked over the

179

gate. He could see now that it *was* a dog, and it was certainly the biggest dog in the world. It had an enormous head, and a gold coat that really did look like a lion's. One more WOOF was enough for Jeremy James. His legs started spinning again, and away he went as if his tricycle was a rocket.

'Nothing to be frightened of,' said Daddy. 'Big dogs are just little dogs at heart.'

'Big dogs,' said Mummy, 'have bigger bites than little dogs. I don't think it's fair for these people to let their dog out like that. Jeremy James won't be the only one he'll scare.'

It was therefore decided (by Mummy) that Daddy should go and have a word with the new neighbours. Jeremy James went with him on his tricycle, and as they drew near to the house with the high hedge, there was a loud WOOF and Daddy jumped. The next moment, the garden gate opened, and out came the lion-dog pulling along a tall man with a bushy grey beard.

'Easy, Leo,' said the man.

'That's a big dog you've got there,' said Daddy.

'He's a big softie really,' said the man. 'One pat and he'll be your friend for life.'

He turned to Jeremy James.

'You want to give him a pat?'

Jeremy James didn't want to give him a pat. Jeremy James wanted to give him a wide berth. If Daddy hadn't been there, Jeremy James would have rocketed away as fast as his legs could spin.

'Good boy, Leo,' said Daddy, and rather

tentatively stretched out a hand to pat Leo's mighty head. Leo poked his tongue out and said something like: 'Ha heha heha heha heha heha!'

Just then a lady came out of the house. She had dark hair and glasses, and smiled when she saw Daddy and Jeremy James. The bushy-bearded man, whose name was Mr Scott, said she was his wife, and then Daddy introduced himself and Jeremy James, and Leo went on poking his tongue out and saying, 'Ha heha heha heha heha heha!'

Jeremy James had now eased his tricycle close up to Daddy and within patting distance of the dog.

'Stroke his head, Jeremy James,' said Mr Scott.

Jeremy James stroked Leo's head, and Leo looked him straight in the eye and licked his chin.

'Yuck!' cried Jeremy James.

Mrs Scott laughed. 'He likes you!' she said.

Jeremy James wasn't sure that licking and liking were the same thing, but when Leo sat down next to him and pushed his head forward for more stroking, Jeremy James was finally convinced.

'Mind you,' said Mr Scott, 'Leo doesn't do that for everybody. He only licks nice people.'

Daddy and the Scotts walked together to the supermarket, while Jeremy James cycled on ahead, holding Leo's lead as the animal trotted beside him. He didn't really look like a lion at all now. He just looked like a big soft dog.

A few days later, Jeremy James set out for the sweet shop again. (He went to the sweet shop at least once a week.) As he drew near to the house with the high hedge, there was the usual WOOF, and Jeremy James stopped to pat Leo on the head before setting off again on his tricycle.

The sweet shop and supermarket were around a corner, and Jeremy James had just turned it when he found himself confronted by two very rough-looking young men. One had long brown hair and was leaning against a dirty white van, and the other was stubbly and had a cigarette in his mouth. The stubbly one stepped straight out in front of Jeremy James, so that he had to stop.

'Well, well, what 'ave we 'ere?' asked the stubbly man.

'Looks like a brand-noo tricycle,' said the long-haired man.

'Cost a lot o' money those do,' said the stubbly man.

'I'd like a tricycle like that,' said the long-haired man.

'It's not new,' said Jeremy James. 'I had it last Christmas.'

'Did you?' said Long Hair, pushing himself off the van. 'Then maybe it's time you got rid of it. Ask Mummy an' Daddy ter buy you anuvver one.'

'Off yer get,' said Stubble, and grabbed the handle-bar.

'No,' said Jeremy James.

'Wotcher mean, no?' growled Stubble. 'Gerroff before I knock you off.'

'Leave my tricycle alone!' cried Jeremy James.

''Arry, lift 'im off, will yer?' Stubble said to Long Hair.

Long Hair immediately grabbed Jeremy James under the arms and lifted him out of the saddle.

'Let me go!' cried Jeremy James, and waved his arms and legs as hard as he could, but Long Hair was far too strong for him, and Stubble picked up the tricycle to put it in the van.

'Stop it!' cried Jeremy James. 'Let me go!'

At that moment there was a sudden patter and a growl and a blur of gold. Stubble's face turned white, the cigarette dropped from his mouth, the tricycle dropped from his hands, and he let out a word that Daddy had once used when he hit his thumb with a hammer, and Mummy said Jeremy James must never, ever use.

Long Hair let go of Jeremy James, and there was a loud thump and an even louder cry as a dog as big as a lion leapt straight at his chest and knocked him down onto the pavement.

'Gerrim off, gerrim off!' screamed Long Hair, as Leo stood over him snarling and growling, with teeth bared as if he was going to eat him.

Stubble let out his naughty word again, then ran to the door of the van, jumped in, and drove away.

Meanwhile, the noise had brought Mr Drew out of his sweet shop, and several people had come out of the supermarket.

'Gerrim off!' yelled Long Hair again.

'What happened?' asked Mr Drew.

'They tried to steal my tricycle,' said Jeremy James, 'but Leo stopped them.'

184

Mr Drew went back into his shop to ring for the police, and the people from the supermarket stood around while the long-haired man screamed for help.

'That dog could kill him,' said an elderly man in the crowd.

'No! Don't let him kill me!' yelled the long-haired man.

'Serves him right,' said a grey-haired woman.

'I never meant no 'arm!' yelled the long-haired man.

'Someone should get the dog off him,' said the elderly man.

'Who's going to try?' asked a lady with a shopping basket.

'Please, please gerrim off!' sobbed Long Hair. 'I promise I won't try an' escape!'

Jeremy James went up to Leo, and there was a gasp from the crowd as he put his arms round the dog's neck.

'Good boy, Leo,' he said. 'Good boy. You can get off him now.'

Leo stopped growling, stepped off Long Hair, and sat down quietly as Jeremy James stroked his head. But when Long Hair tried to move, Leo growled at him, and so Long Hair lay flat on the pavement again.

Just then Mr and Mrs Scott arrived, and Jeremy James explained what had happened.

'I saw him jump over the gate,' said Mr Scott, 'so I knew something was going on.'

A moment later, they all heard the sound of a siren, and a police car drew up beside the pavement.

'So what's goin' on 'ere, then?' asked the policeman. (It was his brother who had cycled to Jeremy James's car boot sale.)

The crowd parted to let him through.

'Oh, it's you, 'arry, is it?' said the policeman. 'What you lyin' down for?'

Harry started to get to his feet, but Leo growled so Harry lay down again.

'Take me away from 'ere!' he cried. 'Before 'e kills me.'

Harry confessed his crime, Jeremy James told his story for the third time, and the policeman said the other man's name was Mick and he wouldn't get far.

Everybody agreed that Leo was a hero, and the elderly man said that Jeremy James was a hero too.

'He saved your life!' he said to long-haired Harry.

'That's true,' said the lady with the shopping basket.

But Harry didn't even say thank you.

Mummy and Daddy were quite shocked when Jeremy James got home and told them the story, and Daddy went up the road to thank the Scotts and – especially – Leo.

There was one thing, though, that puzzled Jeremy James. He'd already gone round the corner when Harry and Mick had tried to steal his tricycle, so how could Leo have known that he was being attacked?

'Dogs are very clever,' said Mummy. 'They often know things that we don't.'

Some people say that dogs are a bit like children.

CHAPTER TEN

The Wedding

Tim and Lisa were getting married. Tim was an old friend of Daddy's, and was very tall and as thin as a match. Lisa was an old friend of Mummy's, and was very short and also as thin as a match. They were a good match for each other. At the wedding, Daddy was to be best man, and Jeremy James was to be a pageboy.

'What *is* a pageboy?' asked Jeremy James.

'A pageboy,' explained Daddy, 'is a boy who . . . um . . . well . . . pages.'

'You'll have to follow the bride,' said Mummy.

'Where to?' asked Jeremy James.

'Into the church, and up the aisle,' said Mummy.

'Can I ride my tricycle, then?' asked Jeremy James.

Mummy said tricycles were not allowed in church – even tricycles with bells – and Jeremy James would have to walk.

The wedding was to be a posh one, and Daddy and Jeremy James would have to hire special clothes for it. These clothes were known as 'a nuisance'.

The other thing Jeremy James would need was a

new pair of shoes, because his old ones were a bit too shabby to go with the nuisance.

'I'll need a new dress too, John,' said Mummy. 'And a new hat.'

'Jeffer new dwess!' cried Jennifer from the playpen.

'Quite right, darling,' said Mummy.

'Kwiffer new dwess!' cried Christopher from the playpen.

'He's getting funny ideas,' said Daddy.

Jeremy James and Daddy went to a special shop in town, and were fitted out with long black coats, dark trousers, frilly shirts and red bow ties. After the fitting, Daddy took Jeremy James to a shoe shop, where they bought a pair of black, shiny shoes, which Jeremy James was not to wear until the day of the wedding.

The evening before the wedding, Daddy and Jeremy James had to go to the church. Tim and Lisa were there, and so were two little girls who were to be bridesmaids, and an older girl who was to be chief bridesmaid. The Reverend Cole, who was very old and rather wobbly, greeted them all with a very serious face.

'A terrible tragedy,' he said. 'I'm so sorry.'

'What's happened?' asked Tim.

'The death of your father,' said the Reverend Cole.

'My father died fifteen years ago,' said Tim.

'Good heavens,' said the Reverend Cole, 'you've waited a long time.'

'What for?' asked Tim.

189

'The funeral,' said the Reverend Cole.

'What funeral?' asked Tim. 'I've come here to get married.'

'Really?' said the Reverend Cole. 'Aren't you Colin Johnson?'

'No, I'm Tim Davies,' said Tim.

When the Reverend Cole had put away his funeral book and taken out his wedding book, he explained what everybody was supposed to do. Jeremy James was to follow the bride and bridesmaids up the aisle, carrying a little cushion on which would be two rings. At a signal from Daddy, he would sit down with Mummy and the twins, and at another signal he would carry the cushion to Daddy, then sit down again. When the wedding ended, he would follow the bride and bridesmaids out of the church.

What really interested Jeremy James, though, was the bridesmaids' job. They were supposed to carry the bride's train. He was a little surprised that she had a train. And why were trains allowed in church, but tricycles weren't?

'Now, are there any questions?' asked the Reverend Cole.

Indeed there were. And the answers were as follows:

Yes, the bride really had a train; no, Jeremy James could not carry the train instead of the cushion; and oh good heavens, the train wasn't a choochoo – it was the end of the bride's dress.

Jeremy James couldn't see how part of a dress

190

could be a train, but the wedding clothes were funny anyway. Perhaps he could fix his tricycle to the end of his long black coat.

No, he couldn't and, according to Daddy, he had asked enough questions.

The next day was bright and sunny. Daddy took the twins and Mummy (in a beautiful blue dress and hat) to their seats in the church, and then came out again to wait with Jeremy James, who looked like a little lord in his long coat and his shiny black shoes. Tim (also in a long coat) was already there greeting people as they arrived, but he slipped away to get the cushion with the rings.

'Don't drop them,' he said to Jeremy James. 'We can't get married without these rings!'

Jeremy James held onto the little red cushion as if it was the last bar of chocolate in the world, and he fixed his eyes on the rings as if they were the last two liquorice all-sorts.

And so the wedding began. Lisa, the bride, walked beside her father, with her arm resting on his. She was wearing a flowing white dress, which the bridesmaids were holding up at the back. There was no sign of a train, so maybe she'd decided not to bring it after all. Jeremy James followed them, carrying the little red cushion out in front of him. Even before they entered the church, they could hear some loud music being played on the organ: Taa tumtetum, taa tumtetum, taa tumtetum-tumte, taa tatatumtetum . . .

The music continued until the bride was about halfway up the aisle, and then it stopped, and the

191

little procession walked on in silence. In silence, that is, except for one very high-pitched sound. It was a sort of ooeek, ooeek, ooeek, ooeek . . . And it could be heard every time Jeremy James took a step.

Heads began to turn. Ooeek, ooeek, ooeek, ooeek. One grey-haired lady turned pale, and whispered very loudly, 'It's a mouse!' Two or three other ladies wanted to jump up on the pews, but their husbands held them back.

'It's not a mouse,' whispered one of the husbands. 'It's the little boy's shoes.'

Ooeek, ooeek, ooeek, ooeek. The shiny black shoes slowly squeaked their way towards the altar, and a lot of faces began to smile. One or two even began to giggle.

Jeremy James, however, held tight to his cushion and kept his eyes on the rings. As a result, he didn't notice that the bride had stopped, that the bridesmaids had lowered the end of the dress, and the chief bridesmaid had gone to lift the bride's veil. He only noticed when his shiny black shoes got caught up in folds of white cloth and he found himself falling right between two little girls.

The bride felt a sort of tug, and there was a sudden roar of laughter. Lisa, her father, the chief bridesmaid, Tim and Daddy all turned to find Jeremy James lying at Lisa's feet – still clutching the cushion in both hands.

'First of all,' said the Reverend Cole, who had seen nothing of the fall, 'let me welcome you to this happy occasion. It's lovely to see so many smiling faces.'

Daddy – a little red-faced – hastily picked Jeremy James up, and lifted him off the bride's dress.

'It's a particular pleasure,' said the Reverend Cole, 'to see so many children here.'

The chief bridesmaid straightened the bride's dress, and Daddy made sure that Jeremy James hadn't hurt himself and hadn't lost the rings.

'It's the children,' said the Reverend Cole, 'who bring a special joy to these occasions.'

He was surprised by the enthusiastic response to this remark, and resolved to use it again at future weddings.

By now the bridesmaids had sat down, and Daddy whispered to Jeremy James to go and sit in Mummy's

pew. With cushion and rings and a few squeaky
ooeeks, Jeremy James stepped back down the aisle.

'Jem Jem!' cried Jennifer, as Jeremy James sat
down next to her.

'Put the cushion down on the seat,' Mummy whispered, and very carefully, Jeremy James laid it
between himself and Jennifer. The two rings shone
brightly up at him.

Scarcely had he sat down when the first hymn was
announced, and so he had to stand up again. Jennifer
wanted to stand on the pew, but Mummy said it was
too dangerous, and so Jennifer and Christopher
remained seated.

'All things bright and beautiful,' sang the congregation,

'All creatures great and small,
All things wise and wonderful,
The Lord God made them all.'

After that, there was more sitting down and
standing up, and the Reverend Cole talked a lot,
and Tim and Lisa said something that Jeremy James
didn't hear. During a quiet moment Christopher
said 'Kwiffer weewee', and Jennifer fell asleep, but
otherwise nothing much happened. In fact, Jeremy
James had almost forgotten about the cushion
and the rings when suddenly Daddy turned and
beckoned to him, and Mummy leaned across and
whispered, 'Jeremy James, take the cushion to
Daddy.'

It was to be one of the highlights of the ceremony.
The pageboy would carry the little red cushion to the

best man, who would take the two rings, place them on the minister's prayer book, and in turn the bride and groom would place a ring on each other's fingers. Then, and only then, the minister would pronounce them man and wife.

Jeremy James picked up the cushion, and began to walk towards Daddy. The church was hushed. Ooeek, ooeek, ooeek, ooeek. But not even the squeaking could spoil the seriousness of the moment, or the dignity of the little boy bearing the all-important symbols. Only one thing could do that. And Jeremy James noticed it when he had gone about halfway. There were no rings on the cushion.

Jeremy James stopped. The wedding stopped. The world stopped.

He turned back to look at Mummy. Then he turned forward to look at Daddy.

'Come on, Jeremy James,' whispered Daddy.

He had no choice then. After half a dozen more squeaks, he held out the cushion to Daddy.

'But . . . where are the rings?' whispered Daddy.

Tears began to collect in Jeremy James's eyes.

'I . . . I don't know,' he said.

The tears began to fall.

'It's all right,' said Daddy. 'Keep calm, everybody!'

With a swift movement, he slipped a ring off his finger, and popped it onto the cushion. Then he pointed at the Reverend Cole's finger.

'What?' asked the Reverend Cole.

'The ring!' whispered Daddy.

'What ring?' whispered the Reverend Cole.

the bride's father had seen what was happen-
d quickly put his own ring on the cushion.

K, Jeremy James,' whispered Daddy, 'you can
go back to Mummy now.'

With tears falling like a summer shower, Jeremy
James returned to his pew, and a little murmur of
concern rippled through the congregation.

'What happened?' whispered Mummy.

'I've lost the rings!' sobbed Jeremy James.

He and Mummy looked round the pew, and they
looked on the floor, and they looked underneath the
wide-awake Christopher, and they looked underneath
the sleeping Jennifer, but the rings were nowhere to be
seen. They were well and truly lost.

'You must have dropped them when you fell over,'
said Mummy.

But Jeremy James knew that he hadn't dropped
them.

He cried all through the rest of the wedding, and
he cried afterwards, when the church bells were
ringing and everyone went outside to have their pho-
tographs taken. Mummy and Daddy, and even Tim
and Lisa, tried to cheer him up, but he would probably have gone on crying for ever and ever if he hadn't
suddenly noticed something that nobody else had
noticed.

It happened when the photographer called out:
'Best man, bridesmaids and pageboy, please!'

Daddy was carrying Jennifer, who had just woken
up, and as Jennifer was not required for the photo-
graph, he handed her over to Mummy. Mummy

196

out to take her, and Jennifer reached out to 1, and at that moment a bright light flashed nnifer's hand straight to Jeremy James's eye.

ere they are!' shouted Jeremy James.

And there they were. One ring was on Jennifer's thumb, and the other round her middle and forefingers. She must have taken them while Jeremy James and Mummy had been singing the hymn, and then she had fallen asleep.

Tim and Lisa were delighted to get their rings, and said Jeremy James was a hero for finding them. People crowded round, and there was a lot of laughter when they heard the story. Only Jennifer failed to see the funny side.

'Jeffer wing!' she complained. 'Where Jeffer wing?'

'They're not your rings,' said Mummy. 'They don't belong to you.'

And for once Jeremy James agreed with the grown-ups.

A selected list of titles available from Macmillan Children's Books

The prices shown below are correct at the time of going to press. However, Macmillan Publishers reserves the right to show new retail prices on covers, which may differ from those previously advertised.

All Pan Macmillan titles can be ordered from our website, www.panmacmillan.com, or from your local bookshop and are also available by post from:

Bookpost, PO Box 29, Douglas, Isle of Man IM99 1BQ
Credit cards accepted. For details:
Telephone: 01624 677237
Fax: 01624 670923
Email: bookshop@enterprise.net
www.bookpost.co.uk

Free postage and packing in the United Kingdom